Rumors from the Lost World

Stories by Alan Davis

Minnesota Voices Project Number 54

New Rivers Press 1993

Library of Congress Catalog Card Number 92-85452
ISBN 0-89823-142-6
Edited by Vivian Vie Balfour
Editorial Assistance by Paul J. Hintz
Cover Painting by Catherine Davis
Book Design and Typesetting by Peregrine Publications

The publication of *Rumors from the Lost World* has been made possible by
generous grants from the Jerome Foundation and the Metropolitan Regional
Arts Council (from an appropriation by the Minnesota Legislature). Addi-
tional support has been provided by the First Bank System Foundation, Liberty
State Bank, the National Endowment for the Arts (with funds appropriated
by the Congress of the United States), the Star Tribune/Cowles Media Company, the Tennant Company Foundation, the United Arts Fund, and the
contributing members of New Rivers Press. New Rivers Press also wishes
to acknowledge the Minnesota Non-Profits Assistance Fund for its invaluable
support.

New Rivers Press books are distributed by:

The Talman Company	Bookslinger
131 Spring Street, Suite 201 E-N	2402 University Avenue West
New York NY 10012	Saint Paul MN 55114

Rumors from the Lost World has been manufactured in the United States of
America for New Rivers Press, 420 N. 5th Street/Suite 910, Minneapolis,
MN 55401 in a first edition of 2,000 copies.

For Catherine,
and for Sara, and Dillon

When they stirred in their sleep
we fell through the crust
sometimes to the waist,
to the topmost branches

of the trees in which frozen
birds perched,
waiting for the sky to melt.

—Michael Hettich,
from *A Small Boat*

ACKNOWLEDGEMENTS

Some of the stories in *Rumors from the Lost World* were published in different form in the following places: *Arts Journal, Beyond Borders: An Anthology of New Writing from Manitoba, Minnesota, Saskatchewan, and the Dakotas* (New Rivers Press, 1992), *Crescent Review, Denver Quarterly, Fiction Review, The Greensboro Review, Kansas Quarterly, North Dakota Quarterly, Northland Review, Pulpsmith*, and *Roberts Writing Awards*. Our thanks to the editors of these publications.

The poem by Thomas McGrath is from *Selected Poems, 1938-1988*, published by Copper Canyon Press. Used with permission.

The excerpt from *A Small Boat* (University of Central Florida Press, 1990) by Michael Hettich was used with permission of the author.

The author wishes to thank the Minnesota State Arts Board for a Fellowship, Moorhead State University for its support, and Ragdale for a room with a view. The author also wishes to acknowledge Vivian Vie Balfour's editorial assistance and the support of C. W. Truesdale and Katie Maehr, who have done a great deal of work on behalf of this book.

CONTENTS

is anyone
completely here?
—Kathryn Levy

You out there, so secret.
What makes you think you're alone?
— Thomas McGrath,
Selected Poems, 1938-1988

SHOOTING THE MOON

I had baseball cards and books about time travel, my brother Edward had the television, my father double shifts at a factory job, my mother housework and a secret wish for a baby girl. We reached for nothing greater, but my grandfather was different.

Once a week I walked him to the local library. If I got lucky, he entered quietly in his flannel shirt and overalls, waved his black glove, and chose a few books. On the way back to our white frame house, he swung his rubber-tipped cane for balance, the crook on the end like a bishop's crozier. On the front stoop, cuffs tucked over the shoestrings of his work boots, he lit up one of his King Edward cigars. "You kids know nothing. They've filled your head with crap."

He paced his attic room, as foggy as a London street in a Sherlock Holmes melodrama. Cigar smoke swirled away through tiny gable vents and his face with its squints and wrinkles came clear in the flare of a match. He was an atheist and a socialist; somewhere in his book-lined haunt above my bedroom was a newspaper article about George Bernard Shaw he liked to read to me. Sitting on a packing crate, I wasn't able to make much sense of what he read, but it was heady stuff, and I swayed in his rhetoric as his black glove tapped across the page. He wore the black fur-lined glove because surgery left the hand freezing on the outside and burning on the inside. My father was often away nights, working his double-shifts, so my mother trudged up the stairs with a porcelain bowl of hot water balanced against her good hip. Grandpa needed his soak.

Even so, there would have been no heated discussions about nursing homes had he submitted gratefully to this Florence Nightingale act. Her two boys weren't old enough to minister to him, only to listen as she braced the slopping bowl of scalding water and planted a foot on the next step, groaning and gathering a breath, but she appreciated the man who sent me to the corner store for cigars. He gave me tip enough for a box of Good N' Plenty, licorice candies with pink-and-white sugar shells. The man who sat at our formica breakfast table with his magnifying glass, reading quietly for hours, accepting refills of coffee with a professorial nod, was comforting to her. She thought his political opinions were nothing more than the cantankerousness of a man whose favorite team had lost the World Series.

Nothing was further from the truth. When I was unlucky, he worked himself into a rage before we even reached the wooden red-shuttered library. On our final visit there, he scowled at Mrs. Douglas, the front-desk librarian who knew my mother, and vainly searched the card catalog for radical primers. "They've got books in here that make goddamn fools out of people," he said, loudly enough to be heard across the long room. "I don't want my boy here to grow up to be a fool. Do I have to take him downtown to get him a book worth reading?"

After a few minutes of this, Mrs. Douglas got on the telephone, gesturing emphatically, speaking at a staccato pace, and my mother soon arrived in the wood-paneled station wagon. Through the library's plate-glass window I saw her try to parallel park. She wasn't very good at it, especially when aroused. She kept turning the wheel too abruptly. The rear tire kept bumping into the curb. I knew she would lose patience and leave it that way, angled out like a gangplank into traffic.

Mrs. Douglas hovered behind the counter, stroking her chin. It was the gesture she used on any patron who got out of line. "Ruth," my grandfather shouted to her, "why don't you just sit down on your ass and play the fool?" My fingers ticked on the frayed binding of a green *Reader's Guide*. The library was hardly the local hangout, but a couple of my classmates were there, staring oddly in my direction. A middle-aged member of the Ladies' Auxiliary put down the latest popular novel and crossed her arms. Had God (who in my imagination looked something like Mickey Mantle, right down to the pinstriped uniform) entered the library at that embarrassing moment and promised to make the old man vanish, I would have taken cover on the far side of the card catalog and told The Mick to have at it. My grandfather was the kind of straight-backed old man who attracted scorn instead of pity; he would never surrender to reason, fatigue, or even to my mother.

She strode through the door and said something to him in an angry whisper, and even now it's hard to tell what happened in the conventional style of reminiscence. "Bitch," he answered. "You're a little fascist, that's what you are, a little bitch of a fascist, working your husband to death to fill your house with crap." She slapped him so hard he raised his bad hand instinctively. The black glove flew in a small arc and landed five feet away. I picked it up and held it just so by one of its fingers. It felt soft to the touch, as though the fingers had somehow worked it smooth from the inside. Looking at nothing else, I followed it to the back seat of the station wagon, where a cop was placing a parking ticket under the windshield wiper. I tried on the glove, still warm and moist, and cursed the capitalists before losing my nerve and laying it to rest on the seat. My grandfather, face flushed, a welt already showing on his lower cheek, limped past the wagon, his right arm twitching. "Goddamn fascist bitch," he muttered.

My mother wedged herself behind the wheel and stuffed her mouth with a stick of chewing gum. She noticed the ticket and her jaws started working double-time. Without a word, she turned on the wipers. The ticket fluttered to the asphalt. She gunned the motor and whipped the station wagon around, nearly sideswiping a VW bug. The car's owner, opening a door for his wife and child, gave her the finger.

She gripped the steering wheel with one hand, elbow resting on the window well, and waved a cigarette with the other. "I'm sorry you had to see that," she said. "Grandpa's just old, poor thing. He's had his disappointments." She flung her wad of gum into the street, took a deep angry drag on the cigarette. "It's too goddamn much. I'll tell you one thing. He uses that kind of language again, he's gone." She stubbed out the cigarette. "Your father wants to put him somewhere, great. Otherwise, he can live on skid row with the scumbags and loonytunes."

That evening my parents argued in their bedroom below me. "I'll go there first," my father shouted. "That's for people who can't function, who have to be spoonfed, have to be wiped." My mother said something quietly, but in that tone of voice that could vibrate right through you.

"We don't always *earn* our afflictions. Sometimes they just *happen,*" my father answered, so loud I could tell he was drinking. "We want a girl, you can't have more kids. Is that your fault?" They were up and down all night, using the toilet, opening the refrigerator, the conversation flaring up over and over again like a fever. Above me, my grandfather paced out the disturbing rhythm of his own thoughts. He had big dreams as a young man, hoped to go to college, become a labor leader. "He wanted fame and women," my father once said, "never mind the fortune." Something obscure happened, though, something to do with the Great Depression. He ended up spending his life on county roads, repairing watches. Then his eyes went bad and his wife died.

"I like living in the attic," he told me once, smiling for my mother. "It's a quick way to get off the face of the earth." He waved his cigar. "I'm closer to heaven in case of a stroke."

"Where's heaven, Grandpa?"

"It's on the left side of the moon. You can't ever let them shoot the moon. That's where you go for coffee and beans when you're out of luck."

The day after that last confrontation at the library, he came down dressed in baggy slacks and a rust-colored turtleneck that climbed the pale skin of his abdomen. A tattered socialist newspaper under one arm, one white-knuckled hand holding tightly to the banister, he descended upon Edward, my younger brother. Wearing a blue Detroit Tigers cap, Edward was folded fetus-like into the recliner, entranced by a game show.

4

"Turn off the damn television," my grandfather said.

Edward looked at me. I raised an eyebrow in silent complicity, forgetting the yellow smell of the newspaper, the mustiness of the attic room with its narrow metal bed, the sound of that scratchy voice echoing from the rafters. I only remembered how often, under duress, I read a radical primer instead of a book of high adventure, how often my grandfather scoffed at my baseball cards. For an awful minute, I only remembered standing in the library, blaming him because he somehow wasn't what people expected.

Edward, who was no gentleman, doffed his cap like Al Kaline, his hero, after a home run. "Grandpa, sit down and shut up."

"All right," he said, to my amazement, and sat on the sofa. He pulled out a cigar and tore off its tip. "We'll watch it together, you and I, we'll see what we can see." I suppose he intended to pontificate on the evils of consumer capitalism, but the whirling wheel of the game show, the incessant detergent commercials and the moderator's patter hypnotized him. He fell off to sleep, head thrown backwards, mouth open. Edward planted his cap back on and called my mother. She tried to work a plastic sheetcover under him—he was becoming incontinent—but he woke. "What the hell?" he mumbled, rubbing his eyes. "Where's your husband? He's never home, is he? Too busy filling this goddamn coffin with gadgets."

"Hey, 'Gunsmoke' is coming on," Edward said, turning up the set. Chester, the gimpy deputy sheriff, was trying to keep order until Matt Dillon returned from Topeka.

"Look, this can't continue," my mother said. "Why don't you form your own society or something? I don't see you refusing the food we put on your plate." In fact he ate like a bird, lived on coffee and toast. "Besides, we've achieved everything you've dreamed of."

"But you don't have *dignity*, you don't have *respect*," he said, nodding with conviction.

He tried to retreat to his room, muttering under his breath, but couldn't negotiate the stairs. He sat down on the bottom step, feet planted on the hardwood floor, and covered his face with his hands. "Oh hell," he said. "Oh hell."

When my father heard the story, his face turned an ugly color.

He tossed a few union leaflets on a sideboard. A family portrait, an oil painting, hung a little lopsided on the wall. In it, my grandfather was absent and we were all much younger, smiling like Christians because the painter had been one. "That's it," my father said. "He's brought this on himself. I wash my hands of it."

Even my mother, who devoted so much of her life to keeping things clean, never put it quite that way.

At the Sleepy Hollow Care Center, he had a tiny airy room. Outside his window was a flower garden, part of a public park, in season well-tended and full of salmon colors and greens and blues.

When we paid him a visit, he had nothing to say, just worked his jaw and stared at the flowers.

My parents inscribed his favorite Shaw quote on the headstone, one he repeated often, especially when mocked or contradicted: "Some people see things as they are and ask why. I see things that never were and ask why not." On the day we buried him it rained. I stood in the drizzle beside his grave, staring at the words on the tombstone and daydreaming into the spit-shine of my best shoes until the service was completed. Afterwards, we went for pizza.

Without him in the attic as ballast I floated away, and my mother, after a prolonged but successful quarrel with my father, sent me to Bible School, of all places. Talk about Jesus got mixed up with diatribes about the workers' struggle for dignity, the batting average of Mickey Mantle, and the plot of *The Time Machine*. By the time I went off to college, the thought of that inscription in the cemetery made me cringe.

One cloud-swept autumn afternoon, I told Sally, my wife, about the inscription, expecting her to grin. "A neat old man," she said. "You know that's the quote Bob Kennedy used on the campaign trail?" She nodded, staring from the wraparound porch of the restaurant to a bevy of geese flying south in formation. She had worked hard for Kennedy, followed his every notion in the papers. "How come you never talk about him?"

I stared at her. It was true. After a fashionable renouncement of my family, I decided politics, especially Shaw's creaky socialism, lacked existential truth. I felt profoundly sorry for my grandfather. His illusions had made his life miserable. I shrugged. "You saw what happened to Kennedy," I said, stroking my goatee sagely as geese plummeted through tatters of cloud the color of cigar smoke.

Even long dead, he continued shouting. I'd wake, thrashing upstream in my dreams, to the odor of cigar smoke and attic mustiness. He wanted his story told, he wanted someone to listen to an account of his ungentle passage through the world, but instead of sitting my wife down and talking until I got hoarse, until vocal fry punctuated my memories, I'd take off my glasses and palm my hands over my eyes, then journey to a lake cabin with a redwood deck. Stones dropped into clear water, making concentric circles. My grandfather sat beside me, rocking on the porch. I have his weak eyes, you see, use them as much as he did. In another exercise, my eyes open to the darkness inside my hands, I saw him walk past me, swinging his rubber-tipped cane, staring at the fence, the cow-pasture finish to our deadend street. He hooked the cane on a strand of barbed wire and climbed. On the other side, he paused, surveyed the high grass, gathered a breath and went on, into a field of black-and-white cows.

"How can he be dead?" I said, finally telling her the story one late afternoon. "I can still *see* him. He's still there, sitting at the kitchen table, pinching off the tip of a cigar, quoting Shaw or Carl Sandburg." All afternoon we had sandpapered our bedroom wall and spackled nail holes, getting it ready for a new coat of paint. The cigar-smoke color of the paint as I rolled it onto the walls, or maybe the intoxicating effects of its fumes, set something off in me. I couldn't stop talking. "So I stood in a hard rain beside the grave," I finished, "wearing my best boots, and then we went for pizza."

"Boots? You wore boots?" Jaunty after a job well done, she grinned. But it was clear she had listened, really listened. "Somehow I can't imagine you in boots."

"Shoes. Okay?" I clicked my tongue, a little irritated. "You find the rhythm of the story, a few details change. The point is, I had something on my feet."

"Sure," she said. "I get it." Then she furrowed her brows. "*Pizza?* You went for *pizza* after a *funeral?*"

"Yeah," I said, and bit into my lower lip. "What's wrong with that?"

"Nothing." She shrugged. "We have to eat, I guess. In respect for your grandpa, though, I hope you skipped the anchovies." She

7

put down her putty knife and went off to rinse her hands with turpentine. When she returned, her mood had changed. "No, look, I'm sorry. Really. I'm sorry he was so unhappy." She rubbed her eyes and sniffed her knuckles, as though ready to cry. "If it's any consolation, your father was right, I think. We don't earn our afflictions. Sometimes they're just given to us, we have to live with them."

That was it. My grandfather was alive in somebody else's head, the head of someone I loved, and I knew she would keep him there, tell people about him from time to time. Air him out, so to speak, let him move through the world in a way which was still very difficult for me. She smiled, shrugged, and padded into the kitchen to start dinner. I worked on details in the bedroom, touching up the baseboard, smoothing out the rough spots, but by nightfall the job was finished, the paint mostly dry.

I joined my wife. Candles were flickering on the dining room table and the good china was laid out like a message from a more perfect world. Sally had pulled out a silver wine bucket, a wedding gift forgotten for years, and filled it with ice and a bottle of *vin ordinaire,* the only sort of wine we drank. After dinner, we brought the candles and the last of the wine to the new room and toasted my grandfather. The room was pale gray and satisfying to sit in, like being a child again and walking with him to that red-shuttered library on an overcast afternoon, his mind filled with the plight of the workingclass, mine with the necessity of traveling back and forth in time.

RAMPARTS STREET

E mily, after rejecting the eighties and its gold-plated bait, has
come to the idea that she can learn about herself and her times
by learning about her mother, getting in touch with her roots.
Emily even flirts with taking a course in Italian, a language her grandfather spoke with gusto. English, though it served him well enough,
never gave him pleasure. He liked to roll Italian phrases in his mouth,
feel how they forced his lips to puff out and pucker with male pride.
In English, he was much diminished.

For Emily's sake, her mother tells and retells the story of a rainy
February evening in 1942, when two government agents tore apart
the house with carnival glee, as though Mardi Gras, which vanished
with the war effort, had to be replaced with something more physical
than periodic blackouts and air raid practice, the self-important warden
with his metal hat and flashlight smirking as he lectured the nineteen-
year-old girl. "A single match could give away our position, sister."

Emily takes the story to heart, cites chapter and verse. "You were
an American, Mama, New Orleans born," she says, rubbing her fingers
together like her father. "You went at things the way your ancestors
did, hardscrabbling, getting in the door without asking. Isn't that
what the Vietnamese are doing, the Mexicans, the Cubans, the
Haitians, all the immigrants?" Emily gave up managing a health spa
in the suburbs of New Orleans to work with displaced people. "The
same people who want to keep them out are the ones whose fathers

9

wanted to keep us out, at least until they learned how to use us as strikebreakers. And now they want to cut the capital gains tax and give another break to people who don't need it. Isn't that right? Am I getting it right?"

In response, her mother swirls her teaspoon in her coffee-and-milk. Each time she tells the story, she manages to recall more of the truth of what happened, because, God knows, on that overcast February evening she couldn't explain herself the way she can now, after chewing it all over for so many years.

"But you were valedictorian the year before the war started. Isn't that right?" Emily says. "You gave the commencement address. You knew a thing or two."

Whatever, her mother says. It was 1942 and Mama motioned me close. "Come upstairs, child," she told me, though I was a high school graduate, already rebelling against the social constraints my father insisted on. "I don't want them going through the tin box." This was World War II, remember, fought so long ago people called it The Good War? Against the Germans, the Japanese, the Italians. Errol Flynn came once to the Municipal Auditorium to sell war bonds.

"It's a scream," Emily says. "You know I'm right, don't you? New Orleans has always been the country's salad bowl. Greeks, Italians, Irish, blacks, French, Spanish, Eastern Europeans. You name it. The whites thinking they could do what they wanted to blacks, the Irish and the French thinking they were better than Mediterraneans. Am I right?"

Well, her mother says, we saw newsreels of the Blitz, used ration stamps, had to line up for meat, sweeten our coffee with saccharine, do without ice cream and cake. We knew something was wrong. Patriotism seemed like the answer. Anyway, I couldn't figure why Mama wanted the box hidden away, but no matter. I was obedient. It was GI green, about the size of a breadbox, full of our papers. Birth certificates, death certificates, marriage certificates. A world in a breadbox. And my father's alien registration, paperclipped to a miniature Italian flag—those bright sun-filled colors, so different from the war effort. You know we had to mix bright yellow food coloring into the margarine to make it look edible?

I shoved the box into my closet, because the two agents downstairs, even though they were tearing our house apart, wouldn't search the room of a girl, an innocent daughter. So Mama figured, anyway, leading me back downstairs. "Not a word," she said. "Not a peep."

At nineteen, I was the youngest of thirteen children born to Mama, and the only one who still lived at home. It was a Tuesday, I remember, a meatless Tuesday, and Olsen was as thick as a steak, a good half foot taller than me. He slit open a sagging chair, the one in front of our gramophone, a console bought second-hand and polished to a high mahogany sheen. The chair would be worth maybe a dollar on the street, but it was the one nobody else sat in when Papa was home.

"You toiletface," I said. My mother put a hand to her mouth, my father started grinding his jaw, but he was afraid to speak. It was the first time in my life I used such a word, the worst I could think of, though God knows I heard it often enough, something my brothers called my older sister. But the effect was different, a little scandalous, very vulgar, in the mouth of a bashful child, five foot two. I was no bigger than Charlie Chaplin. "What right you have to come in here?"

"Every right in the world, sister," Olsen said. Grinning, he pulled one of my long dark braids. "That's some head of hair you got, sugar." He looked over at my father, sitting stiffly at attention, perspiring in his frayed, worsted suit. "We're just making sure you all cooperate with the war effort." He slashed the chair until stuffing came out, then overturned a steamer trunk. Worn keepsakes, sweaters, shawls, and doilies spilled across the floor.

Seeing red, nothing but the motion of my blood, I rose to my toes and pummeled Olsen in the back. "You damn palooka!"

Shoulders hunched, he pivoted, frowning, and took one long steady look before bursting into a low-registered laugh. Gasper, the second man, came up behind me and hoisted me to the couch, sat me down with my parents. "That's enough, Joe Louis." My father, jaw grinding, studied the frayed carpet in that self-conscious way people have when they're embarrassed for the furniture. As for my mother, she was no Sicilian, but she knew what poverty was. She also knew we were just a bad break from more of it.

"They put up with that shit?" Emily's face gets puffy with anger.

She snaps open her purse and digs in it, as though searching for the cigarettes she no longer smokes.

What could we do? her mother says to her, staring at chipped china, drip-drying in a wire drain next to the sink. New Orleans was a military center. Soldiers all over the place, Army hospitals on the lakefront, Nazi subs at the mouth of the river. We were supposed to roll bandages, knit socks and sweaters, save tinfoil and coat hangars, old license plates. There was the rationing, the blackouts. We didn't know we had any rights. Olsen and Gasper had official business, they said. "Why do you have a radio but no transmitter?" Olsen said. "Where's your transmitter? You have a short-wave?"

"We listen to Beethoven," I said, "but you wouldn't know him, would you?"

"He's a dago. Who else would you listen to?"

"Beethoven?" Gasper furrowed his brows. "He's not Italian, is he? Verdi, that's your man. You listen to him, sweetheart?"

"And Caruso. We listen to Caruso. You wouldn't know him, either. You're stupid."

My mother squeezed my knee with a large-veined hand. "Just be quiet."

"What are these questions, Mother?" my father asked in his heavy English, his long big-boned face twitching a little, his downturned nose engraving sadness onto his features. He required me strictly to be home by ten, allowed chaperoned dates only, and suspected my volunteer work at the USO. He forbade me to attend late-evening get-togethers, especially dances for servicemen. He didn't trust soldiers with his baby, and the more I argued the darker his face became, like the skin of an eggplant. "I have every right in the world to go to that dance," I had been screaming, almost in tears, when the two men knocked.

Outside it started to rain, a sudden gale from the gulf. Winds thirty miles an hour, the tops of big oaks waving like people adrift in lifeboats. It was better than Beethoven, those storms. Before the war, I'd sit by the window, lights out, the night turning off and on, sheets of rain plinking the glass, the ballgame droning on the radio for my brother's benefit, sheet-lightning punctuated by shouts of victory or disgust. When the war came, he got sent off to the European theater, where he met one of his heroes, a pitcher from Mississippi.

"Look, Mister," Gasper told my father, who was running his watch-chain through his fingers like rosary beads, "we're fighting fascism. You should be glad we're vigilant."

"Yeah, right," Emily says, retrieving one of her own father's butts from the ashtray and breaking it apart.

Fascism? For all I knew, Olsen was a fascist. He was certainly dressed for it in his wrinkled, shiny black suit. He pulled out a cigarette, without permission to smoke, tapped it in his palm, and struck his match. "What's a little discomfort, a little annoyance, compared to freedom?" he said. "You all don't know how good you have it. Suppose you were still over there in that stinkhole? You think you'd get a place like this to feel at home in? You think you'd get all that good Spam to eat when there wasn't enough meat to go around?"

My father studied the jiggling glint of his watch-chain.

He had the shakes. When he was little, I found out later, his parents spoke of innocent men dragged by dead of night to stakes in the scorched uplands of Sicily, where predators and insects and the sun would kill them. In America, it was rumored that the government relocated people into prisons in the desert, that Italians were never safe from a beating or the kind of grilling that convinces you you're guilty.

"If it's not our country, too," I said, "then what's my brother doing over there? Why don't you send him home? He's fighting for his country."

"Which country is that?" Olsen said.

"Olsen," Gasper said. "That's enough." He furrowed his brows again, bushy, gray things like caterpillars, and walked to our tiny picture window.

"The point is, sister," Olsen said, "they're not in Italy. They might have some trouble with that."

"When we get to Italy, they'll be there," I said, "protecting a coward like you."

Olsen turned to my mother. "You got any coffee? How about a little hospitality here?" He sat next to my father, in the spot my

13

mother vacated when she went for the coffee. "Where's your registration papers, old man?"

"This is his country," I said. "He's been here since he was a kid. He's been here forever."

Gasper, staring at the rain, turned from the window. "I wish that was true, sweetheart. The truth is, I'm sorry about this, but he was born overseas, he never naturalized. There's a man here who says he likes Mussolini."

"Who says he likes Mussolini? Mantegna? Was it Mantegna? That's a lie."

"Maybe that's true, sister, maybe not, but how come he never naturalized?"

Even today, Emily's mother doesn't know for sure. He was born in 1877, came by boat to America. He was still a child, spoke Italian for years, part of that huge melting-pot immigration that filled those aging sway-backed houses in the French Quarter chock-a-block with Italians. His parents grew produce in Kenner and opened a small grocery on Ramparts Street. He learned English waiting on customers. It wasn't a bad life, certainly an improvement over the arid soil of Sicily, the scourge of absentee landlords, the life of an indentured farmhand. In South Louisiana there was rent, hard backbreaking work, French Creoles and Irish who called them dagos and worse, there was the heat. But it was paradise compared to Sicily, where bandits and bloodshed in the uplands restricted travel one way, while the fertile coast had nothing for peasants. America had always been a bright shining dream.

"Where the rich get richer," Emily says.

Anyway, he couldn't explain to the men why he never naturalized, though he tried. He made box-like gestures with his hands and clawed at the air, reaching for something tangible, something plausible, as though kneading dough, but finally shrugged the question away. "I have my papers," he said.

"Well, why didn't you say so? Let's see them," Olsen said. He waved at the mess in the living room. "Nobody likes this, but it's like a hurricane. You don't want it to happen, but it just does. It's nobody's fault, you understand. It's like that rain outside. You don't make a big deal about a rainstorm, do you? That wouldn't do nobody any good." He leveled his gaze at Papa. "Especially the people waiting out the storm."

"I know where the papers are, you big jerk," I said. "I'll go get them."

My father sat very still, as though posed for a picture. He was terrified. That I could use the language I did without a stern reprimand was evidence enough. Imprisonment, deportation, the loss of his family. He was uncharacteristically paralyzed. How it must have shamed him, his own daughter going up the stairs for the tin box, Garibaldi-proud, his watch-chain still jiggling in his lap.

Upstairs, the tin box wouldn't open. Mama had the key. I sat on the edge of my bed, defeated. It was a standard-issue tin box, though, and finally I shrugged and carried it before me, hands outstretched, like something intended for the Church. Maybe it was all an elaborate Carnival hoax, maybe the box was full of trinkets. Maybe I'd walk to the top of the stairs with an armful of beads and doubloons and everyone would laugh at our little joke, scream out the classic Mardi Gras refrain: "Hey, Mister, throw me something!"

Downstairs, my mother was serving coffee and cinnamon toast. Coffee was a precious commodity in wartime, hoarded for special occasions, and the cinnamon was pre-war.

Gasper smacked his lips.

"You like that?" I said.

"Your mother's a saint," he said, sipping hot coffee with chicory. "Those the papers?"

"Give it to me," my mother said, "sit down." I put the tin box on her lap. She took a key from a single large pocket stitched to her plain dress and opened the box. On one document I saw the embossed stamp of a notary public. She slipped the registration from the box, leaving the flag buried among other official notices that our family existed.

Gasper studied it, rubbing his eyes, then turned to my father. "So, you used to live on Annunciation Street."

My father smiled for the first time all evening, sensing something in Gasper's voice that passed right over me. Earlier, almost in tears because he refused to admit my volunteer work at the USO was part of the war effort, I had to bite my tongue and sit on my hands. Now I sulked, suddenly quiet, but nobody noticed. What had happened down here when I was upstairs, staring at the magic box whose contents might save us so much trouble? Does coffee and cinnamon toast make such a difference? The key to the adult world, the world I wanted entrance to, was the size of the topsy-turvy room I sat in, and it was a room full of lunatics.

Outside, water dripped from the gutters, splashing on the long, slick leaves of our elephant ear plant. I smelled coffee and cinnamon on my mother's breath. She wants a glass of wine, I thought, reading her mind.

"Salaparuta," Gasper said. "Where's that?"

My father's hands went into motion again, an artful improvisation to conjure up language. "Western Sicily," he said. "Near Gibellina, Ninfa, Belice River. Le isole, siamo cosi buoni." We are so good-natured.

Gasper smiled and nodded. "All right, then." He tugged at his rumpled coat, dark under the armpits. Olsen stood too, pulling at his crotch. "What about that gramophone? There's something funny about it. Should I take a look inside it?" He caressed the dark mahogany.

My father stiffened, but Gasper placed a hand on his partner's shoulder. "Let it go. We've got other business." He turned to my father. "Good evening."

"Auguri infiniti e buon Viaggio," my father said heartily, clasping Gasper's hand, as though consummating a business deal. Infinite good wishes and a good journey. He caught me studying his face and stared for a moment at the broguings on his wingtips. After that night, I never had quite so much trouble getting out for USO dances. I didn't see him anymore as the domineering Sicilian he tried to be, or as the helpless immigrant he was that rainy night, but as a man, one who could be cajoled, who loved the world and its chicanery.

My mother's jaw was set, though, the squiggles around her eyes as taut as wires. "It was none of their business," she said. "Those papers are personal." The idea of a brown-edged piece of paper with an official stamp being personal made no sense to me. Through the picture window, the asphalt glistened like dark soil. Olsen and Gasper walked under the streetlights to their car, Olsen with a notebook in one hand. I could see him stand beyond the elephant ear plant, the great wheeling shadows of its leaves washing over him. He unclipped his pen, made a notation, and pointed down the street.

Emily, leaning over the sink, staring into the backyard at begonias, snorts out a lungful of air. "Did Grandma even ask those goddamn jokers for identification?" Emily shakes her head sadly. "I can't believe you all let them get away with that shit. They might have been thugs—plenty of those around, just like in Italy. Am I right about that? Or maybe they were just vigilantes. You know, entertaining themselves, having a little fun, the way men like to do?"

You let it drip-dry for years, her mother tells her, the anger gets shaved away. Nowadays you think the only important thing is placing blame or realizing yourself, a woman coming to herself, but there's so much water under the bridge. V-J Day on Canal Street, church bells, whistles, horns, people screaming their lungs out. Air conditioning, television, the Superdome, the bridge over Lake Pontchartrain. Nothing was ever the same after the war. Well, live and let live. I do know I carry some sort of history in my bones. Mama died in 1947, I got married in 1949 to your father, Papa died in 1953. A heart attack. At the hospital, they wouldn't give him oxygen until the doctor arrived. By then he was dead and I was seeing my own blood again, screaming at the head nurse. "You goddamned Olsen!" I remember screaming. They sedated me. When I woke, your father was there. He wanted to know who Olsen was.

"It's early enough, Mantegna's shop is still open," Mama said that night, forcing some coins into my hand. "Go get us some flowers."

"From Mantegna?" I said, confounded by what I was hearing. "The jerk who caused us all this trouble?"

"You don't know that," Mama said. "Now go."

I got a bunch as bright as the Italian flag. I walked back to the house under that February sky, where clouds were mountains in the moonlight, and moss hung from live oaks like witch-hair. Louisiana became the sky and the trees, not the shops or the swaybacked houses, certainly not Olsen or the government. I even had to fight an impulse to jump on the trolley and light out for the USO dance. Back home, my father was asleep, or at least alone up in his room, but my mother was hard at work with cleaning rags, threads, and a needle, with antimacassars, old sheets, and a shawl, putting things back together. Manic after my errand on the wet romantic streets, I walked to the top of the stairs with the flowers. "Hey, ma'am, you want me to throw you something?" I shouted, my voice a little too bright, like a waxy apple.

She straightened, the barest flicker of an exasperated smile fighting against her mood, and I tossed the bunch down to her, flower by flower. One for Elizabeth, who died in 1914; one for David, 1922; one for Robert, 1936; one for Frank, Jr., 1939, one for Thomas, who was still alive, but who would die in the war, in 1944; one for Anthony, who died the year after my mother, in 1948; one for Leonard, who had three strokes and passed away in 1959; one for Louis, who was institutionalized for years before a fatal heart attack in 1979; one for Richard, whose liver gave out in 1983; one for your Uncle Joe, one for your Aunt Mary, another for Aunt Emily, your namesake, and one for me. One for Papa, one for Mama, who gathered them all up and found a vase.

I wasn't even twenty when all of that happened. Now I'm close to seventy. Time flies, doesn't it? That wartime night, though, when I was still nineteen, I remember I turned on the radio. While Mama filled the vase with water and bright flowers, the radio filled the room with scratchy big band music. So I jitterbugged, working off my anger with twirls and acrobatic maneuvers. Had Papa seen me, the USO would have been history. Mama stared at me for a minute, not exactly smiling but with her full lips a little lopsided. That was a kind of victory. Then she motioned me over and we got to work again, syncopating our business to the quick tempo of jazz.

THE EVICTION

T im took off his jacket. "They're evicting a man across the street," he said. The wind whistled between his teeth and he squeezed his arms, rubbing out April air still too unpredictable to trust, though it promised a journey to a warmer place.

Russell hoisted himself from the couch where he had spent the afternoon and pulled open the venetian blinds on the only window that faced the street. Four men and a woman worked their way down the stairs with a battered chest of drawers, an old flowered couch and a television set. The man they were evicting had on military fatigues and a pair of earmuffs—its metal strap was wired across his bald head like a brace.

Even from the window, where Russell's breath made puffs on the pane, the bald man looked in boisterous good health, leaning against a fire hydrant, big gut slopping over his pants, fingers uncurling and curling. Next to him stood a tall man with a clipboard, in a windbreaker and baseball cap. He nodded as the bald man spoke, then turned away to invoice odd pieces of furniture near a pickup truck on the curb.

"What a thing to do to a man." Tim scratched at his chin. "You think that guy has a place to stay tonight?"

"Tell you what. I'll check it out. I haven't been outside all day."
He came over and put a hand on Russell's arm. "You all right?"
"Yeah, I'm all right."

✳

"Looks like you're getting evicted," Russell said to the bald man.

"Yeah?" He folded his arms and leaned back against the hydrant. "You're a piece of work. You make a habit of coming on to people like me?"

Russell pointed across the street. "You see that window, the one on the third floor with the flower pot?"

"That your place?" He rested his hands on his belly and pursed his lips.

"Sort of."

"Sort of?" He took off his ear muffs, leaving a red slash across the top of his head. Russell was using a medication which increased hair loss, so the shining dome fascinated him. It looked polished. It reflected a little of the late light. "How much room you and your wife got?"

"I'm staying with a friend on a temporary basis."

"Ah." The bald man studied the flowerpot with more interest. "You making an offer, or what?" The man with the clipboard moved away. Two of his workers were horsing around. They looked like the sort of kids who make a little money with temporary work, and the other two looked like drunks. The woman sat in the cab of the pickup truck, motor running.

"We've got a sofa," Russell said. "It's good for one night."

The man with the clipboard, his head a little cocked, turned toward them. He waved the clipboard. "I'll give you a hundred for all of it." He removed his baseball cap and stared into the sky. The streetlamps winked on.

"What you say to that?" the bald man asked.

Besides the couch, the chest of drawers and the television set, which actually looked like a good one, there were assorted odds and ends, a cardboard box, a sleeping roll, and a knapsack. "Keep the sleeping roll and the pack, take the money. It's a fair offer."

"That sound good?" the bald man asked.

The man with the clipboard put on his baseball cap and held out his hand. "Deal." He counted the money. Behind him, a blue neon cross blinked from the corner building. Big block letters proclaimed that the building was the home of Our Redeemer Universal Church. The woman in the truck smoked her cigarette and studied herself in the rearview mirror. While the crew packed the truck she put some kind of cold cream on her face. One college kid grumbled to the man with the clipboard.

"Can I help with anything?" Russell said. "You want me to carry that box?"

"This is my filing system, amigo." The cardboard box rested on his gut as they walked. Russell heard things moving around. "Nobody touches it. Nobody. That's why I won't stay at the church. They'll separate me from everything I own. They don't know the information in here could bring down whole governments." He jiggled the box. "Including our own."

Tim opened the door. "Make yourself at home," he said. "They've been evicting people all over the city. Everything's becoming a god-damn townhouse."

"You don't know what the hell you're talking about, old man," the bald man said.

Tim's pupils got bright. "What's that you say?"

The bald man walked to the refrigerator. "You know why they gave me the heave-ho?" He popped open a can of beer. "Because I told those sons-of-bitches they could chew on my ear all day and they wouldn't get squat. That place wasn't fit for roaches."

Tim's mouth dropped open. Face cast into a glower, he pursued the man. "You mean you got money?"

The bald man sized him up. "No, old man, that's not what I mean. I mean I have experience. I've been to Spain, I've seen the bullfights." He swigged down his beer. "I've been to Ethiopia, I was in the Nam for four years. That was a hell of a long time ago. Since then I've been everywhere you've ever heard of and some places you haven't." He walked over to Russell, ignoring Tim, and thumped him on the chest. "Where *you* been, amigo? You ever been to the Nam?"

"The name's Russell," he said. "I've been at loose ends."

"Is that right? Loose ends?" The bald man picked up the phone. "Look, I'm gonna order some pizza. There's a place down the street that delivers."

"You up for pizza, Russell?" Tim asked, concerned.

"Why not?" He nodded to the bald man. "Pizza. With everything."

When it arrived, the bald man paid for it and spread some newspaper on the coffee table. "Let's catch the news while we eat," he said.

"I haven't read that paper yet," Tim said.

"So. You haven't read the paper." The bald man screwed up his face as though working out a problem in calculus. "I tell you what, amigo. Let's leave this paper here to protect the table. It's nothing but ads, anyway."

"You don't seem to understand," Tim said. He picked up the pizza and folded the paper. "You're a guest. You don't tell me what to do."

"Look," Russell said, "let's turn on the TV and see the news."

Tim squatted down to adjust the set. The bald man sat on the couch with his arms outspread and his feet resting on the coffee table, nearly tipping it over. "So tell me, amigos." He grinned a big, goofy cartoon of a smile, his mouth stretched preternaturally wide, his bad teeth sucking in the light. Something gold glinted in his mouth. "Why the Good Samaritans?"

"What's your name?" Russell asked. "You haven't introduced yourself."

"Fair enough," he said. "Jordan. Robert Jordan. You want me to believe you don't know that?"

Tim and Russell looked at each other. Tim got everybody a beer and they ate the pizza. A woman, a reporter, stood on the manicured lawn of a Georgetown mansion. "The two delegates are due to arrive in an hour, to meet with several hundred supporters of their war. Almir Lopez, the chief delegate, will then proceed to Capitol Hill to talk with a group of representatives who favor increased aid."

"That's old news," Jordan said, licking cheese from his fingers. "I know Lopez: a rapist, a murderer, a pervert. I could tell you stories that would uncurl a pig's ass."

"I'd believe them," Tim said, friendly again. "I've heard those people are thugs. We shouldn't give them a cent."

"Those people just want their country back," Jordan said. "Same as the Nam. You namby-pambies were smoking dope and grooving to the Beatles or some shit like that, you didn't have the guts to do what had to be done over there." He leaned forward. "Listen, old man. I've been there. I'm talking from experience, I'm not bull-shitting."

"Look, I'm not up to quarrels. Let's change the subject," Russell said. "So. You don't believe in Good Samaritans?"

Jordan stared until Russell looked away. "Where's the bathroom?" He pushed himself up and rubbed his belly. "I need some Maalox."

Russell pointed to the hallway. "Look in the medicine cabinet."

"You think it's a good idea to let him poke around like that?" Tim asked. They had a stash of marijuana behind the towels. Sometimes Russell would smoke to feel better.

Jordan touched him on the arm again when he returned. "Who the pills for?"

"They're mine. I've been sick."

"That's tough luck." He studied Tim's sparsely-furnished apart-ment, the couch and TV, the two easy chairs, a desk near the win-dow, a dinette set by the kitchen. His eyes settled on a framed photograph of a plot of land with an ocean view, some Spanish land Tim's grandparents once owned. "Myself, I've only got the gout." He placed a hand on Russell's shoulder. "During surgery I contracted blood poisoning. That precipitated it. A goddamn dirty scalpel at a clinic in Bhaunagar, on the Gulf of Cambay."

Tim frowned. "The gout?"

"The gout, old man." Jordan made a steeple with his fingers and bowed. "I suppose you think you know about the gout, right?" He smiled. "About your boy here, though. How long does he have?"

"What makes you think he's my boy?" Tim said. "He's sick, that's all. He's having some tests. What the hell you up to?"

Jordan went to the refrigerator for another beer. "That land on the wall," he said from the kitchen. "Whose land is that? That your land, Russell? Or does it belong to the old man?" Change clinking in his pockets, he belched and sat next to Russell on the couch. His eyes moved a little loosely in their sockets.

"Listen. We wanted to help you out," Russell said. "We also wanted to engage you in conversation. I'm sick and I'm bored. If you don't want to call it a good deed, just call it boredom."

"Forget it." He gently touched Russell's shoulder and yawned. "Look. I haven't slept in three days. Why don't I sleep?" He laid back his head.

"Hear what he's saying," Tim said. He picked up the folded newspaper and slapped it on the coffee table. "I don't like this kind of bullshit."

Jordan opened his mouth in surprise and crossed his eyes. Then he was out like a light, even beginning to snore. Tim looked at Russell, who knew Tim was gauging how difficult it would be to drag the bald man to the door, how much trouble it might take to call the cops. "To hell with it," he finally mumbled.

Russell went to the spare bedroom. Later he dreamed about an old Mediterranean pension. There was bougainvillea, a patio, a tile roof the color of deep rust. From the patio he could see water. A man in bathing trunks brought him a tall drink. "Will there be anything else?" he asked. "Sit with me," Russell said. "I can't go inside, I have to study the water." The water changed color several times each day, he had to see the changes. It changed from the color of bluebells to the stained green of military fatigues, then darkened at night to ink.

When Russell came to himself, Jordan was in his room, sitting on the far side of the bed. For a moment, still almost asleep, Russell closed his eyes and expected his mother to clatter early-morning dishes or his father to sing in the shower. Russell had gone to western land-locked Canada instead of Vietnam and didn't come back until it was safe. That broke things with his father. His father told him once he couldn't show his own face at the main street cafe in the small town where he lived because he didn't want to have to fight the man who called his son a pussy. But Russell never forgot how his father sang in the shower. His throat would gurgle on low notes, straighten out, then lose its way as it climbed the scale.

Jordan ticked a fingernail on a water glass jammed between his legs. "I thought you'd never wake up," he said, voice full of beer.

"What time is it?" The smell of beer and pizza mingled with the odor of Russell's own perspiration. "Where's Tim?"

Jordan pulled a penlight from a cargo pocket. "You decided to be *kind,* is that it?" He played with the penlight, pointing it at the ceiling, flicking it off and on. "I would hate to think, *Russell,* that I'm the beneficiary of your goddamn pity. If there's one thing I don't need and won't stand for, it's goddamn pity." Spidery lines sprouted around his eyes, he smiled without any humor, his jaw locked and teeth clenched. His mouth sagged, each breath a little struggle. "I've got something I want to show you," he said, and pulled out a billfold, stained to the color of soil. He waved it in Russell's face. After digging in it, as though it were a diplomat's pouch as large as the world, he handed Russell a grimy faded snapshot, worn thin like onionskin. "My boy," he said. "I've got a boy, too."

It could have been a likeness of Jordan's own face for all Russell could tell. Even the original snapshot before its careworn travels must have been faint, like the image a ghost-hunter might point to as evidence of something everyone around him smirked at.

"No hair, just like his old man," Jordan mumbled. He laid his head on Russell's chest. The bed squeaked under his shifting weight. Russell had trouble breathing. "Jordan, get off my chest," he said, as loudly as he could, the ache in his lungs beginning to spread down to his liver and legs.

Jordan was falling asleep like that, settling into Russell's kidneys, when Tim thudded open the door with the heel of one hand and switched on the light. "What the hell? Russell?" Russell motioned for help. Tim grabbed Jordan by an earlobe and forced him to a sitting position. The empty tumbler was still wedged between Jordan's thighs. Jordan hefted it to eye level and turned it in the light. Drops of beer flickered like beads of glass. With a quick flip of his wrist, Jordan tossed it away and it thumped against the baseboard near the door, clunked across the worn carpet without breaking. His jaw dropped open. "Goddamn. Your glasses don't break."

"Look, buddy, it's almost light outside," Tim said. "I want you out of here. Off to the bullfights."

"The bullfights?" Jordan said stupidly. "What the hell you saying? I need some sleep."

Tim pestered him like a turnkey until Jordan collected his things quietly, as though sleepwalking, and left, tossing a bill on the sofa and snapping off a last goofy smile in Russell's direction. "Hey, amigo," he said, "no hard feelings."

Tim crumpled up the bill and threw it out the window at Jordan. Then he stood with Russell, who was leaning into the night, breathing in the crisp, chilled air. "You know what?" Tim said. "That buttface walked off with my goddamn newspaper." Tim closed the window and stared at his own fading reflection. "I'm not that goddamn old, am I?"

"No. I'm just as old as you are, speaking in real time." Russell kept looking into the street. Elbows akimbo holding the box, Jordan walked away bowlegged, his pack jiggling in blue blinking neon. "You're no older than anyone your age. It was just his way of getting to you." Later, when he was alone, Russell noticed the nail on the wall, the one the picture of Spain had hung from. The empty space was two shades lighter than the plaster around it, but the land and the water, rustling somewhere in Jordan's box, is still a place Russell can close his eyes and go to.

GROWING WINGS

Diane stopped using her full-length mirror when the small white feathers on her back were large enough to see from across the room if she twisted in her nightgown like a dancer. Close up, the feathers were invisible, the angle of vision all wrong, so she turned the mirror around and stared for hours at its black paint. She also made retreats to a large utility closet full of baggy flannel shirts and large woolen socks. In class, sitting against the back wall, she wore a faded gray trenchcoat to hide the feathers, but her teacher, Mrs. Hanes, often made her hang it up in the coatroom.

She stared at a waterstain above the classroom door. Jamie, who always sat next to her, leaned close and whispered something. She failed to respond to him or to a question from Mrs. Hanes. "Pay attention," the teacher said. Diane lowered her eyes to the worn floor, pockmarked with swirling wormlike scratches. *We should learn not to be aware of ourselves,* she had read that morning in her sister's spiritual notebook, *to no longer have ideas, but to simply live what we are.*

"Diane, redeem yourself. What's the theme of *Lord Jim?*"

Her pennyloafers scraped circles on the tiles, a muffled rhythmic whisper. *You tend to interpret everything, an internal conversation goes on always in the mind.* She repeated Melinda's polished phrases for the comfort. *You must open yourself to the possibility of not-thinking, or meditation, as it's commonly called.*

"Diane!"

Jamie poked her gently. She looked up. My sister often wore purple, she thought; it's very spiritual.

Mrs. Hanes got the students writing. "Come with me, Diane."

In the principal's office the steady hum of an air conditioner sounded like the whisper of shoe leather on tile and she thought about the Salvation Army store. Her mother would be scandalized to know how much time she spent there, off the beaten path her classmates followed to school, but it was comfortably musty with a smell of wool and mothballs. The woman at the store always let her sit quietly, often next to a wheezing air conditioner on its last legs, and she would listen to Melinda's voice. *We see what we want to see. We don't see things as they are. We have to discipline ourselves, watch the motes of dust in the sunlight, learn how to put such discipline into effect.*

Sometimes the woman gave her a glass of milk. "You ever talk, sweetie? Or do you just sit and think?"

For the first time Diane told someone. "I'm growing wings."

"Oh. Well, that's good, I suppose."

"I need an overcoat. Do you have one?"

"Oh, I think we might." The woman smiled, her breath sweet with Feen-a-mint gum. She fitted Diane with a coat a size too large. "It only costs a dollar today, wings or not. A special."

A hand placed itself gently on her shoulder. The principal. "Don't you listen, Dee?" He guided her to the counselor's office, his hand still on her shoulder like a small friendly animal. "I'm to leave you with Mrs. Esposito, to have a talk."

The door closed. "Hello, Diane."

A pause. "Hello, Diane."

A longer pause. "Well, we don't have much to say today, do we?" *The Universal Law resolves everything, but there is always a tendency to be impatient,* Diane thought, still feeling the warm weight of the principal's hand.

Mrs. Esposito adjusted a small gold pin on her tweed jacket and shuffled through a manila folder. Violet nail polish, Diane thought. Why did she choose that color today?

"Now, let's see. You were just here, when? Last week? Yet here we are again, and you're still wearing those silly clothes. What's the story?"

Diane leaned forward. "Is something the matter with your eyes?"

"My eyes?" Mrs. Esposito picked up a small mirror. "My contacts, maybe? They seem okay, but let's look." She closed her eyes and gently massaged each eyelid.

"How's that?"

"Better."

"Hmmm. Well. Tell me, how much time do you and your mother spend together? Does she have much time for you since your father and sister passed away?"

Experience is a flash of lightning in a sky filled with dark clouds. She visualized the words as they appeared, neatly copied in her sister's elegant script.

"Dee? Did you hear me? What's the story?"

Diane smiled. "I'm fourteen years old." She held up both hands, fingers spread wide. She closed her hands and then displayed four more fingers, two on each hand.

"Yes, I know." Mrs. Esposito folded her hands over the notes and waited.

"It's my mother. You're right."

"Yes? What about her?" The counselor motioned for the girl to continue. "You can tell me, Dee. You can say anything. Nothing gets past these doors. I'm safe as a bank."

"Well . . . "

"Yes?"

"Well, my mother . . . Look, I don't know how to say this, Mrs. Esposito. But Mother, well, she eats tennis balls."

Mrs. Esposito's face reddened.

"It's the truth." Diane crossed her heart. "It's driving me bananas. But what can I do?"

"What do you mean, 'eats tennis balls'? What's that supposed to mean? Does she spend a lot of time at her club?"

"No, just what I said. She uses ketchup, mustard, sometimes a slice of onion. And on the *good* china, Mrs. Esposito. Can you believe? It's disgusting." She pointed to the telephone on the desk. "Please call her right away and tell her to stop."

After Mrs. Esposito dismissed her, Diane walked through the empty hallways. Classroom voices discussed dangling modifiers and the Civil War. Words filtered into her awareness and fell away to vague murmurs. Drone City, she thought, and looked up. Sorry, sister, I'll get serious. Then she giggled, remembering the expression on the counselor's face.

Her trenchcoat and floppy hat waited in Mrs. Hanes's classroom. She overcame a desire to feign sickness or maybe just go home and settled instead for the comforting silence of the lavatory. The low hum of fluorescent lights, the coziness of dull porcelain and laminated particle board stalls made this the one place where she could stop thinking without fear of reproach. *They've told me I won't have to come back here again. This is the last time I'll have to go through this.* The words had the graininess of chipped marble, as though written on the wall before her. She stretched and turned to the mirror, twisted her neck and noticed how her flannel shirt bunched up near the shoulder blades.

✳

"What happened in the office?" Jamie asked on the walk home. "They didn't kick you around, did they?"

There was a layer of sky above the one where most people stopped looking. She always had at least one ear cocked in that upward direction. I'm becoming better at walking toward each moment without interpreting anything, she thought. But if I don't listen with discernment, I'll miss Melinda's call when it comes. She saw Jamie frown. "Are you happy?"

"Huh?" Jamie shrugged. He looked down at his feet. "I guess."

"You ever pay attention to the way you walk?"

"I don't know. Not really."

"You ought to."

"I guess. You don't, um, pay attention sometimes." He stared down the street to her house. "By the way, you want to walk to the park before we go home?"

"No. Not today. I don't have time. Thanks, though."

"Oh. What else do you have to do?"

"I grow wings." She looked at him appraisingly.

"Oh. Wings, huh? I grow hair." He smiled.

They reached her house. "Well, good-bye, Jamie," she said. "Thanks for walking with me."

"Did you wink at me?" he asked.

She giggled. "Are you happy?"

"Sure. I'm glad you winked. Didn't you wink?"

"It doesn't matter. See you later. Be happy."

✳

The sounds of dusk became clear, as though traveling across water. Diane sat on the front porch, her feet propped on the railing, leafing through Melinda's notebook and eating a banana sandwich. Eyes closed, she saw her sister talking in a slow hypnotic voice about the long spiritual struggle to leave behind the chains of the world, to climb cold mountain slopes. The dreamy voice brought Diane to the edge of trance, but willing her sister's appearance was more difficult. A car door slammed. Chords of practice exercises started up on a piano behind lacy curtains across the street, and then voices in the drive. Her mother stepped to the porch, holding an unlit cigarette. "Hello, kiddo. You get something to eat?" No reply. "Jack and I are going to a movie. You want to come? It's a Burt Reynolds thing, a romantic comedy. But we got to leave soon to make it."

"Okay. Have a good time. Don't eat too many tennis balls."

"Huh?"

"You better take it easy on the onions, Mother."

"Sometimes you're too silly to believe." She puffed on the unlit cigarette. "I don't have bad breath, do I?"

"Only when you frown, Mother." She riffled the pages of the closed notebook, still carrying a faint suggestion of patchouli. "Mother. Did Melinda ever grow wings?"

"Huh?"

"Wings on her back?"

"Wings? What you saying, kiddo?"

31

"Wings, Mother. White, with feathers. Flap flap." She dangled her arms to illustrate.

"I still don't understand." She tapped her cigarette on the porch railing. "Stay in the real world, kiddo. It's all we have these days. Right?" She glanced at her watch. "Hey, you sure you don't want to come see Burt Reynolds?"

"What do you mean, 'the real world'?"

A large dog, fenced in, barked fiercely at a passerby. It was Jamie, shuffling past. He waved feebly and put his hands in his pockets, shoulders slumped. The car door slammed, her mother and Jack drove away. Alone, she realized how much she missed Melinda, whose presence always calmed her, like Sunday mornings stroking the veneered pew in church, daydreaming through stained-glass windows, absent-mindedly mouthing hymns. Across the street curtains parted briefly to reveal the profile of the young piano student. *All actions should be spiritual manifestations. If approached with the right motivation, it is fine to have all sorts of actions and experiences, even distractions, but not to attach to them.* Diane smiled. Maybe the piano student secretly flapped her arms like wings, became a black crow and flew, squawking.

She lay on her bed. Were her own wings a sign from Melinda? Or rather, what kind of sign? Maybe she too had lived many lives, and had to be here only this one last time. In the light of a single candle shadows played on the ceiling. An owl chased a pumpkin, the owl became a cactus-flower, the cactus-flower became a pumpkin. The thunder of an airplane turned on car headlights that slanted through the window, illuminating a hanging fern, which in turn shed a tangle of waving fingers on the ceiling. A huge brown bird wearing her overcoat grabbed her. She fell in Jamie's lap, he kissed her, she reached up, touched her sister's lips. And woke, thirsty, uncomfortable, back aching, on the verge of tears. Don't think, she thought, and blew out her candle. There were places, she decided, remembering her wings and turning to her side, where she wasn't ready to go. One of Melinda's books, *Spiritual Initiation,* urged the apprentice to maintain detachment, discrimination, discernment, the three keys to interior serenity. But she couldn't relax. Why did dreams of flying frighten her so? Why did Jamie, in her dream, become Melinda? Was she ready for wings?

✳

"Go to the counselor's office for your appointment," Mrs. Hanes said several days later. Distracted by Jamie, Diane stared at the floor, where a black ant made its deliberate way to a crumb.

"Young lady!"

She grabbed her coat and hat as she left.

✳

"Dee, please take off that ridiculous hat," said Mrs. Esposito.

"If you take out your eyes."

"How can you hear me with that stupid thing on?"

"Excuse me. What did you say?"

Mrs. Esposito lit a cigarette. She wore a neatly-tailored suede jacket, dark green, which Diane wanted to caress. "You can be so sweet," she said after a long puff, "but you're in one of those moods, aren't you? What's the story?"

"There's nothing to be done." Diane stared into swirling smoke. "There's nothing to be done and nowhere to go."

"That's a ridiculous thing to say, isn't it, Dee? I mean, where would we be if we all thought that?"

"Nowhere."

"Exactly. Nowhere. We can't give up, can we?"

"You don't understand."

"Well, maybe not." The counselor stubbed out her cigarette. "You know, Dee, you haven't had much to say to me. Have you? Melinda died last summer and we still haven't talked about it. Is there anyone else you talk with?"

Diane touched her forehead. "What does this have to do with anything?"

"I don't know, maybe a lot. It depends what the story is." She reached across her desk. "Take this glass of water, for instance. I would say it's half full, but someone else might call it half empty." She sipped

33

water and cleared her throat. "Look, Dee, it's not nice to have a father or sister die, much less both, and especially when it happens all of a sudden. I've had that happen."

"You had a sister die?"

"Well, no, I was an only child, but my father died when I was twenty, and my mother not so long ago." She stroked her chin. "They were sick, granted, and we expected them to go, but that didn't make it easier." She picked up a ballpoint pen and clicked it. "I only want to help. If we can monitor these automatic thoughts you have, maybe we can figure out some sort of rational response. Your thoughts affect your feelings, and then your feelings control your thoughts. It should be the other way around."

Diane breathed deeply. "What makes you think I need help?"

"Mrs. Esposito leaned forward. "The way you get sometimes. The way you are right now. The way you react to my questions. You do want to talk, don't you?"

Suddenly Diane pulled her floppy hat over her eyes and lowered her voice an octave. "I have the trenchcoat. Don't you think I should ask the questions? Where were you on October fifteenth?"

"Come on, Dee. What's the story? Let's get down to brass tacks."

"Okay. You smoke cigarettes. Aren't you afraid of cancer? Think about it."

Mrs. Esposito smiled tightly, pulling back her lips into a line. She glanced at her watch. "Of course. You're right. I should give them up. Anyway, it's time for the bell. You think about it too, okay, Dee? We'll keep seeing one another for a while, or maybe we can find somebody else to help."

*

"Did you hear me in class?" Jamie asked.

"No."

"There's, um, a dance tomorrow night. It's in the gym. Want to come?"

"No. I don't think so. But thanks for asking, Jamie."

"You don't like dances?" Jamie kicked a divot out of somebody's lawn. "Me neither. What I mean is, what else you have to do? I mean, we can do something else."

She picked up a leaf and pressed it carefully into the pages of her book. "I told you. I grow wings." Why was she telling him again? It was secret.

"Oh." Jamie frowned. "That's interesting. And I told *you*, I grow hair. You know we all have the same amount of hair? Only some of us have it inside our heads and some of us outside."

Diane laughed. "That's funny, Jamie." He glanced at her and she giggled. "You don't believe me?"

"Oh, sure. Can I see?"

"No. Definitely not. Why you have to see? You can't take my word?"

"Yeah, I guess. But I let you see my hair."

"Let's forget about it. You have expectations, don't you?"

"What do you mean?"

"Think about it."

"Why should I think about it? Why can't you tell me?"

"Are you happy?"

"How can I be happy when you won't tell me?"

"That's what I mean."

✳

She tossed in bed that night, tried to lie still, but her body was taut, wings larger. And she didn't feel comfortable on her stomach. She turned on the bedside lamp and the curtains ruffled in a slight breeze. She listened for crickets, but it was too late in the year. *They've told me I won't have to come back here again. This is the last time I'll have to go through this.* The last time she saw Melinda, her sister had a load of books for the library. "I'll be right back," she said. "You wait up and we'll make banana bread for the orphans." Diane tilted her head quizzically. "Orphans?" "You know," Melinda said, laughing, "the ones on the railroad tracks." Oh, thought Diane, the cartoon we saw.

The memory made her angry. I've seen Melinda since then, she thought. Other people, no, but *I've* seen her. Staring at the well-thumbed notebook, she shook her head stubbornly and turned off the light. The library books, the last conversation, the way Melinda precariously balanced what she said and what she carried. At the funeral, clutching Melinda's notebook like a portable altar, deliberately impersonal, one of the few without tears, Diane was detached, even serene. Mourners descended upon her. "They called for her," she told them. "The death was painful because she could learn something. And my father didn't feel anything." At the wheel, he had a heart attack, the car swerved across the highway's center stripe.

Come to me, she willed, sitting up in a half-lotus position. Instead, Melinda stood painfully vivid before the car with the library books. Okay, sis. I know things don't work that way, but give me a sign. In what form do you watch over me? Make yourself known, I will wait for you here. Her tongue swollen, she dragged herself to the bathroom for water. The light at the bottom of the stairs guided her down the hall, past her mother's empty bedroom, where two glasses glinted on a night table.

She gulped down the water and turned, to go back to her room. Instead, she slipped off her gown and opened the medicine cabinet over the basin. She took down a pair of scissors with blades the color of graphite. I'll trim my wings, she thought, beginning to cry. I'll have baby wings.

AWOL

Y our son's AWOL," the officer told Leon Levoski on the
phone. There was a long silence, some whispering. "He
couldn't hack it. We don't think he's back here, but you
never know with this type of individual. Hell, he could be anywhere.
He might be in Canada, Switzerland, Hong Kong. Hell, he might
be getting off the bus across the street from your house." Levoski
heard a rasping cough, the unmistakable whisper of a match close
to the speaker.

The officer's flat monotone lay for weeks like too much whiskey
on his chest, and now, wife in tow, he was drinking off his despair
at the Stardust, a dive in Chicago Heights. Strips of braided foil danced
in heating ducts. Mistletoe and holly fluttered over the doors. Colored
lights winked from the bandstand, where The Memphis Hound Dogs
covered Elvis songs. The overwaxed dance floor was empty, but two
bleached-blonde women on the far side of forty, both tall, both pan-
caked with makeup, swayed at the uncrowded bar. They were lost
in erotic contemplation of the singer and his greasy ducktail. The
taller woman had a beauty patch penciled on one cheek. As she swayed
under a fluorescent tube, the patch seemed to crawl up her face.
Levoski stretched his own features into a contemptuous leer.

"What the hell, Marge," he said, reaching for the pitcher of beer.
"The trouble with life is, everyone stays home on Christmas Eve."
When he rose, the blood rushed to his cheeks. Marge stroked the

thin dark fabric of her dress and reached for her coat, draped over their booth. The Elvis clone whispered "Love me tender" into the mike, then jerked his pelvis.

"Hold your horses," Levoski said. "I'm just going for a leak."

"Let's get home, Leon." Marjorie studied her watch. "Paul might try again. He always calls Christmas Eve."

"For chrissakes," Levoski said. She still didn't know about the phone call. "Let it be. He's not gonna call. Let's just sit here and get goddamn drunk, okay?"

The waitress reached between them for the ashtray and Levoski noticed a dark, ugly mole on her upper arm. "You ought to get that taken care of, honey," he said, touching the mole lightly.

"You a smartass, or what?"

The singer, still grinding his hips, belted into "Hound Dog."

In the near-dark of the small entranceway, Levoski leaned his head against flimsy paneling. He couldn't get a handle on the thing. His own son, a deserter? "Daddy, where are the clouds?" Paul would ask after dark, his voice plaintive, barely audible, his Oshkosh overalls a size too large. "The clouds are still there," Levoski said, frowning. "You just can't see them, kid. Why don't you go out for a pass?" Paul clung to his father's stocky denim-covered thigh. "Daddy, where are the clouds? Where do the clouds go?" Levoski pried the boy loose and waved the football toward the street. "They evaporate. At night they evaporate and go to bed." He tucked the ball under one arm and gave up. "Let's go inside, kid." But Paul didn't give it up. Dressed in jammies, his eyes were still troubled. "The clouds evaporate?" he said. "What's evaporate?"

A couple entered the lounge, letting in a blast of air from the wintry suburban parking lot. The man, in a gray leisure suit, opened the woman's fur wrap and pulled her close for a long kiss. She winked at Levoski. "What's up, big shot?"

He blushed. "I'm on my way to the john."

"M-E-N," the man spelled out. Beneath his metallic jacket he wore a silk shirt and a gold chain. "Right where it's been all night." His face, equipped with a full moustache, stretched tight over his bones. "Don't mind me, my man. I'm real nice once I get civilized."

He held out his hand. "T. J. Raines. *The* T. J. Raines." He nodded to the woman. "And this is Trudy, my nearest and dearest. Let no man rend asunder what Mary Kay decrees." The woman slapped him playfully and pulled on his moustache.

In the bathroom, Raines urinated in fluorescent glare. Levoski, at the next latrine, thought about Niagara Falls, a trick his father taught him, but couldn't forget the woman's low-cut dress, her wink, her throaty voice. Hell, even his mother got loose on Christmas, wore red and green. Looking at Marge, you'd think it was somebody's funeral.

Raines touched his elbow. "*That* never happens to women, you know?" he said. He zipped his slacks and copped a stance before the smudged mirror. "What's your name again?"

"Levoski. Leon Levoski."

"Bond, James Bond." Raines whooped. "Shake it three times, Leo, twice for fun and once for good luck. More than that, you're playing with it." Raines whooped again. His hair was thin, but each strand was carefully water-greased into place, much the way Paul had once done. Levoski's jaws tightened. Something might have happened, maybe Paul was wounded, drugged, unconscious in some alley dumpster, helpless in a jerrybuilt shack.

"My wife's in the bar," he said. "You care to join us?"

In the entranceway, the woman pulled her fur tight around her. "Jesus," she said, "it's cold. What you two been doing in there?"

"Honey, you know how they say *Pepsi's* the pause that refreshes? They got it wrong, sweetheart." Raines laughed. "Anyway, you could've stood in the bar. I was getting to know Leo. Leo likes a good time."

"That so, Leo? You look a little like my first husband, the man I never should have left." She gave Raines a look and giggled, then grabbed Levoski's upper arm. "I need somebody to dance with, honey. T. J. won't dance to save his life. You like to dance?"

Their festive spirits were contagious. Raines got Marge talking about Paul, Trudy hauled Leon to the dance floor. A menagerie of sighs and sexy flutters, her hair all fancy puffs, her black stockings right out of Frederick's catalog, she melted against Leon. The ducktailed singer smirked. "You know I once dated William Shatner? Captain Kirk?" she whispered. "On the dance floor, honey, he'd get as bothered as you."

Levoski blushed. She reminded him of convertibles and palm trees.

"That don't mean you're not worth corrupting, honey." she said as they made their way back to the table.

"After trade school," Marge was saying, "he got with the wrong crowd, repaired diesel engines, and lived with the Incredible Hulk."

Raines tapped his fingers against his shot glass and motioned for another round. "Instead of trade school, you shoulda sent him to one of those *prep* schools."

"Prep school?" She squinted. There were dark circles under her eyes. "Now he's stationed in the Philippines. I'm worried sick."

"He's safer in the Philippines than here," Levoski said.

"The service was your idea, not his." Her laugh echoed high and tinny.

"Come off it, Marge. He made the decision. Anyway, I just wanted him out of trouble."

Trudy reached under the table and patted his thigh. "I wouldn't worry. He sounds like a good kid."

"Anyway, what's wrong with the service?" Raines said. "You ought to be proud." The waitress came to settle up and he grabbed the slip, smiling complacently in a way that reminded Levoski of his father. Levoski protested, but the other man merely winked, and Trudy gave his thigh another squeeze. "Yeah, my man," Raines said, "T. J. always picks up the tab. If it ever comes to the nitty-gritty, I have a whole zoo of people I can eat out on." He rubbed Levoski's shoulder. "Now you're one of them. Where you live, by the way?"

"Not far from here."

He looked incredulous. "You *live* in Chicago Heights?"

"T. J., be nice," Trudy said.

Raines shrugged. "What the hell. Flossmoor's no better. Old fogies waiting on strokes and tumors, giving their cancers a walk every afternoon, taking their bottles of oxygen wherever they go."

"The glamour capital of the world," Trudy agreed, rolling her eyes like Betty Boop. "God protect me from getting old."

"God ain't got nothing to do with it, sweetheart," Raines said, then turned to Levoski. "What you do in the Heights?"

"Roofing business."

"No kidding. Big outfit?"

"Twenty or so."

"Not bad, Leonie. Matter of fact, I need somebody with some good muscle. There's a development I'm looking into, a dump. We're getting permits to put it someplace with no clout. Like the Heights." He flashed a quick knife of a grin. "A lot of business for someone who don't truck with unions. You interested? You won't have to do much *roofing*, you understand."

Levoski, his union card in his pocket, shrugged. "Sure. What the hell."

"Good deal," Raines said, helping Trudy into her wrap. "Put the kid in the business when he's done his time."

"Done his time?" Levoski grunted to his feet.

"Uncle Sameroo." Raines winked. "Your man and mine."

In the parking lot he gave Levoski a business card. "New Year's Eve. Come early, stay late. Meet some people. We'll talk some more."

"I'll be there."

"What's your company, by the way?"

"Midwest Roofing."

"Real original," Raines said, writing it down. Then Trudy rubbed against Levoski for another kiss before the couple disappeared in a pink Cadillac.

Driving home, Leon imagined the words LEVOSKI AND SON painted on the panels of a step-van parked in exclusive Flossmoor. Even in the city, working the steel mills, Levoski had daydreamed about a father-son business. His decision to leave the Works in South Chicago had been provoked not only by layoffs, but also by the dream of that step-van. To hell with working for someone else; he could teach Paul the ropes, tell him small stories.

Marge was dozing, head against the window. Knocked out again. Taking pills for everything from her liver, non-prescription dealies bought on sale at the Walgreen's, to her nerves, little white tablets her woman's doctor gave her by the gross. What had happened since those days when they shared five rooms with his parents? The bells would ring at St. Michael's and they would worship. The rest of the week, he and his father put in time at the mills. Marge, pregnant with Paul, stayed with his mother. She didn't have much energy even then. Red mill dust covered everything, gases from furnaces and coke ovens settled in the lungs like the croup, and their bit of a neighborhood known as the Bush was packed like a sardine between great heaps of burning slag, rail lines, and the belching stacks of the Works. The air tasted like mildewed socks. Even now, Marge hated the place, but Levoski missed it. They couldn't have stayed, though. The Bush was hell in a handbasket. His parents dead, no overtime, crazy fools who would pull a knife on you and strip off your shirt as soon as say hello. Just like every other goddamn place—Levoski's mental map of Chicago was a patchwork of ghettos and tiny enclaves of civilization. Otherwise there were expressways and a thin strip of safe passage along the lake.

At his house, a small bungalow, the glare of the streetlight cast a metallic sheen over asbestos siding and khaki-green shutters. Marge stumbled to bed and he poured two fingers of whiskey. Outside he could hear bottle rockets whine, dogs yelp. Beyond the dim moonglow of his gunmetal gray stoop were duplexes, small bungalows like his own, and apartment buildings decorated with wreaths and strings of colored lights. It looked pretty, the one time of year people pretended the place wasn't a dump. A tricycle lay deserted on the lawn next door. Paul had been a young freckled child who liked to look too long at things, study the way a train moved or the queer arthritic walk of the priest. It's the truth, Levoski thought. He joined the service for me. "All right, I've done it," he said one evening, hair cut close. "It's done." A few mornings later, single bag packed, he left. "Over the ocean," he said. "The other side of the world. See you." Levoski, teeth grinding, put down his newspaper, stiffly walked to the door, stood on the stoop until his son drove away, then climbed a shaky wooden ladder to the roof and worked until his eyes stung.

On New Year's Eve, he fingered the pebbled texture of Raine's business card and decided to continue the patchwork job he started the day Paul left. He gathered up his coat from the living room chair where he had tossed it the night before. Marge was in a trance, staring at her pictures, the soaps, talking back to the screen as though the men and women acting on it could hear her anxious shouts. On the roof, his scalp itchy with sweat, he fidgeted with each granulated shingle, trying to lose himself in the routine, and thought about his father. The old man lived and died with the unions. The union and the trumpet, that was his life. Even when he lost his wind, he kept the instrument shiny, endlessly told the same stories abut playing for Roosevelt once in the service band. He started Leon on lessons early. Too early. One day Levoski left the brass instrument in the practice room and went to play dirtball.

He climbed down from the roof, leaving the job unfinished. In the kitchen, holding down his shirt so it wouldn't ride his belly, breathing raggedly, he poured an orange juice over vodka for Marge. It's time to tell her about Paul, he thought, but she was dozing on the couch, a bony elbow shielding her eyes. On the TV, hundreds of people sang in perfect harmony. Each one wanted to buy the world a Coke. He turned off the set and covered her with an old knitted shawl.

That night, in Flossmoor, the tree-canopied streets were unlighted. Levoski, a little drunk, looked across wide lawns and finally parked near the curb behind a string of Cadillacs and Chryslers. At the lighted entrance, a stocky man with a glistening forehead waved them in. Marge, squinting in the kitchen's bright art deco fluorescence, took a chair, and Levoski went looking for the bar.

The feel of large spaces, of infinitely receding rooms, each a showplace, possessed him with an illusion of grandeur. Several couples were dancing deliriously around a huge fireplace to a frantic beat blasting from the entire wall. Above the fire, two lovers in an oil painting were having one another. In the dining room two men butted heads, the glass table shoved to one side. They snorted and pawed on white plush carpet. A stuffed elk above a tiled bar stared at a buffet loaded with hors d'oeuvres. Through a picture window Levoski could see a covered pool and a tennis court.

The roofer had been in such places, but only to present a bill or accept a cup of coffee. Now he helped himself to whiskey and looked for something sweet. As he jiggled mixers, one of the head-butters stumbled into him, draped a perspiring arm around his shoulder, massaged his collarbone. "Why do I do it?" he asked, a smile plastered on his face.

"Got me," said Levoski.

The head-butter stroked his carefully-trimmed moustache and studied Levoski's two drinks. "You have a woman here? What's she like, this woman? Where is she, this woman of yours?"

"Later." As he turned to pick his way through a cluster of people, an ill-tempered growl was his only warning. The head-butter smashed into his lower spine, nearly flipped him backwards. His whiskey slopped into his face, the orange juice with its dose of vodka drenched the white carpet. He picked himself up, red-faced, and to the sound of scattered handclaps and hoots took a step towards his attacker, who was tramping back to the bar.

Trudy swatted him on the rump. "Losing your balance?" she said. "Don't bother with Vinny. He ain't worth it. He's supposed to fix drinks, but he's loaded. Come on, honey, I'll fix you up." In a half-bath under a stairwell near the front entrance she tended to his wounded pride by sponging his face neat of whiskey. She wore the same silk dress that hugged her figure with such abandon at the Stardust. "Don't worry. You're going to have a great time." She rested a hand on his back. "Come on upstairs, we'll get a fresh shirt."

T. J. Raines stood in the large open-beamed room. "You two looking for something?" He fingered his gold chain. "Or what, my man?"

"T. J., be nice," Trudy said.

Raines belched, turned away from Trudy, and squinted into the fireplace. "Sit down," he said to Levoski. "I'm surprised you had the guts to show up."

Levoski sat on an ottoman. "More fun that bowling," he said, ill at ease on the round cushion.

"Bowling? Like you mean bowling?" Raines leaned forward and launched an imaginary bowling ball into the fireplace. "A ball with big holes in it. Beer. Greasy burgers. Leagues. Unions, right?"

"T. J., be nice," Trudy repeated.

"You're still here, sweetheart? Scram."

Raines sat in the plush easy chair that belonged with the ottoman. "I thought we had an understanding." He fondled a leather pouch of pipe tobacco. "You told me you'd consider a little deal. You told me you owned the company."

"I didn't say that," Levoski mumbled, too sober to find his voice. "You assumed it." He ran his fingers over the ottoman's furred upholstery.

"Assume? You break that down, little man, and you know what it does? It makes an ass of you and an ass of me." T. J. Raines allowed himself a brief smile, then turned and spat into the fireplace. "What you think? I couldn't check you out? You think money grows on trees? You take me for some kind of chump?"

"I just wanted a break." At home in the Bush, he would sink into the old sofa and finger its vinyl iron-on patches, speechless, found out in some petty lie. His father lectured him, accompanying each point with the tap of a finger on an open palm, as though spanking a tiny boy. "You skipped practice, you left that cornet lying in an empty room. You know how that makes me feel?"

"A break?" Raines said. "You set me up, I'll break both your goddamn arms, I'll break your goddamn neck. You force my hand, big guy, and I can be a real swinging dick."

He laid down his pouch of tobacco and opened both hands, as though bestowing a blessing. "Look, boy, I just want you to know I checked you out. I don't give nobody the business without good reason, and I mean that any way you can take it." He stood up and grinned, his face melting almost miraculously from something Corleone might fear to an aw-shucks deference . "You're my kind of schmuck, Leo. Now that you know what kind of meat I'm made out of, we might be able to work together anyhows. " He turned his back on the roofer and shot his cuffs towards the fireplace. "Look, I thought you were hitting on me, taking me for a Rufus. Now I see I was wrong. You're a good man, aren't you, Leonie? Working stiff, barely pays his bills. Am I right, Leonie? You just don't know how to bullshit a bullshitter. Play your cards right, I might be willing to teach you."

Trudy walked into the room. Levoski, red-faced, took the business card from his damp pocket and tore it in half. Raines turned and shook his head cheerlessly. "Don't be a fool. If I thought you were a total moron, I'd con you out of your shirt. But I think we can use each other, my man. Besides, I like to help poor buggers crawl out of the gutters."

"Baby, don't be mean, you really have a mean streak," Trudy said. "Anyway, they're waiting for you downstairs."

Raines picked up his pouch of tobacco and emptied it into the fireplace. "Damn stuff is stale," he said. He gave Levoski's shoulder a squeeze. "What's up, my man? You're not ready to party? Have some fun? Isn't that what we're here for, why we're on this good earth? For fun? Or did you want Trudy to set you up with fingernail polish?" He smirked. "She sells that Mary Kay crap, you know."

"It's not crap, goddammit," Trudy said. "Besides, what paid the mortgage last month, your stock market crash or my troop of ladies?"

"Come on, leave her alone," Levoski said, still sitting heavily on the ottoman, but coming out of his stupor. "What are you, some kind of attack dog?"

"Witty guy." Raines whooped. "You hear that, Tru? Leo is a wit." He squeezed the roofer's shoulder again. "I'll tell you one thing, though. It's good to see your spirit soar. I'm glad you had the guts to say that, Leonie. Not many talk back to the T. J. Raines."

"Come on, sweetiepies," Trudy said. "Let's party. Be nice, both of you. Give him the business if he wants it, T. J. For God's sake. We're starting a New Year."

"I didn't come here looking for no business."

"Is that right, my man? What you come here looking for, then? Maybe I'm wrong, Leo. Maybe you *belong* on somebody's roof. Maybe I'll see you around sometimes." He spit into the now-smouldering fire.

"Baby. Take it easy." Bracelet jingling, fingernails the color of chrome, she put a damp hand on his upper arm. "Remember your blood pressure. Remember your resolution?"

"Yeah, right." Raines turned to Levoski with a boyish grin. "You know how important my blood pressure's become, Leo? I've got a goddamn cuff next to the toilet." He whooped. "Can you *imagine* that? You were a big strapping kid, a football player I bet, a big strong piece of meat. You ever think it might come to this?" He opened his arms wide and puffed out his chest, as though presenting his heart to the room. "Well, what the hell. Make yourself at home. Take a nap if you want. I'm just real sorry I'm moody tonight. When I was a kid, I had a bad relationship with my old man. That kind of stuff gets to you, know what I mean?" Downstairs, people were stomping, clapping, shouting hysterically. "Look, when somebody hits on you, you hit back. It's natural, the way we're made. Kabisch?" He fingered a gold-plated crucifix around his neck. "I've dealt with some sleazeballs, Leo, that's the bottom line. The stories I could tell would make your dick crawl right up into the middle of your face. But I can see I had you pegged all wrong, so let's forgive and forget. One happy family?"

He made muscles with both arms. "It's time for my entrance," he said. "Leo, get yourself composed and come on *down,* join the rest of the animals. I'll see you get exactly what you deserve." Levoski sat very still for a few minutes, working up his nerve, telling himself there was something he had to do, right now, and then he labored down a different set of stairs to the kitchen. Marge was sitting alone in fluorescent glare. "Paul went AWOL," he told her. "I meant to let you know." She stared blankly at him. "You hear what I said? AWOL. Absent without leave. He deserted. They think. Nobody knows where the hell he is, to tell the truth. The boy was a lot of things, but he was never a coward."

"Leon, I want to go home."

"All right." He took her hand.

"I want to go home," she repeated. "Take me home."

"This is a place where a Governor lived," T. J. Raines yelled from another part of the house, "and now it's mine, because I'm *rich.*" His voice turned to the pitch of a barker at a sideshow. "And tonight, tonight we're going to *do* it!"

Great clouds wheeled across the moon. As they pulled into their drive, it cast a fluttering afterglow on the gunmetal stoop. After he unlocked the door and poured drinks for them both, Levoski tried to get hold of some secret. The water of Lake Michigan would be drawn up into clouds. Clouds turn into rain, snow. The same snow on his lawn, soiled by auto exhaust and pages from a newspaper, becomes clear water. It can find its way to Paul on the other side of the world.

Marge sipped her vodka. "Leon, let's get up early and go to Mass. We can light a candle for Paul. We can count our blessings."

Levoski tapped his glass against the picture window. "Yeah, sure. Anything you say." He stared into the street, trying to place her voice. He knew it from somewhere, it was very familiar. So was the neighborhood, duplexes mostly well-tended but only a step removed from nearby apartment complexes, landscaped but weather-cracked, bleak like the projects. A wreath on one door, a plaster-of-Paris Jesus in a picture window.

He saw someone on the sidewalk. Frayed jeans, logging shirt, boots a size or so too large. "Paul!" he shouted, and flung open the door. But Paul had a crewcut, short bristles, and his pale angry face looked like the moon, whereas the features of the dark silent stranger two doors down were hidden by thick water-greased hair. The stranger paused for a moment, even tilted his head, then the screech of a car sent him on his way.

In bed, smelling of dust and whiskey, Levoski held hands with Marge until her steady breathing told him she was asleep. He jostled out of bed. The floor creaked like bones in a dark museum. He knew he would be up most of the night. And there was that patchwork job he vowed he would finish. Working in the cold without sleep would feel like purgatory.

Tomorrow Is My Dancing Day

I n Alabama all roads lead to Tuscaloosa. Believe it or not," the girl's mother says. Perhaps it's that path of least resistance that takes them to I-59, that attracts her mother to the trailer park. To her, it's the average American life. "We'll stay for a month," she says.

Nothing lasts forever, but it takes longer than that to leave. One month of rent, two months of living in with some guy, then something happens. Her mother sniffs it out, and after a week of socking away some money for the road, they force their way past the crucifix tacked to the door. The guy was so religious he wanted to baptize the girl. She told him she wasn't going to no church, especially not on his account, smarting off exactly the way her mother warned her against. "That's okay, honey," he said, his voice nothing but throat. "We don't have to go to any church. I can do it right here in the tub."

Finally their old Chevy squeals from its weedy nest in the trailer park like a motorbike. The guy shakes a fist, fools with his tractor cap until it covers the lines in his forehead, and squints into their dust. "To hell with crap," her mother says. "I'm giving up crap forever. Turn on the radio and *go,* honey, that's our motto. Right, sweetheart? You listening, honey?"

At the cemetery plot, where her mother takes the girl to keep a promise, her daddy's grave is marked with some plastic yellow daisies in a mayonnaise jar. They put them there the day they crunched into town. The flowers are very old, but they haven't lost their color. The girl wipes the petals free of dust with the hem of her long shirt.

An Elvis look-alike is standing one grave over, with his back to them as though waiting for a bus. Her mother flounces her evil eye his way, cracking open her jaw, breathing through her nose like a retard, making the noise a dragon might make until the girl smiles. "Even down to the boots," her mother whispers. "What's he doing here? Why's he waiting on us? You think he's got much cash?" She glances quickly at any gravestone in the vicinity large enough to hide a body behind. In any graveyard, she once told the girl, even the one where her daddy is buried, *especially* that one maybe, she expects the Voodoo Queen or someone alive and grassy to rise from the mud.

The Elvis look-alike seems unaware of them, scratches his scalp and shifts his weight. He's wearing skinny-toed cowboy boots the color of a snake. Her mother is having her fit in slow-motion, leaning over the grave, staring past the dates as though she can't figure them out. "They not gonna change," the girl says. "It ain't a cash register."

"You can say that again," her mother says. "Your daddy was anything but a money machine. He was sure good at laying down and waiting for me to take care of him though, wasn't he? I don't have to go on about *that,* do I?" She leaps like a disco queen to the raised mound where the girl's daddy is sleeping and knocks over the flowers in the process. For a minute the girl cringes, thinking her mother is going into one of her danceplays. The girl's lived with them for years, they can happen anytime, at a pizza place, a motel, a backalley bar, a playground. Her mother pretends she's like listening to the world and letting the world make her move, throwing her arms about, collapsing in a fit, like the Lord's touched her or something even worse.

Instead, she hitches up her skirt and circles the mound as though wrestling with her husband's ghost, then moseys close to the little Elvis. "Boo," she says.

He jumps a mile and a quarter. "Good God, woman, you queer or something? You like to raise the dead?"

She gives him her devil-smile. "Looks to me like the dead's already up and about."

"Sneak up like that in a place like this? Good grief." He don't sound nothing like Elvis when he talks. His voice is high and greasy and quakes a little like it needs to be oiled. He rattles his head, still taking in the sight of the girl's mother in a lowcut T-shirt. His Elvis hair falls into prince charming bangs, straight across his eyes. It's all spruced up and blue so the girl thinks of a blue moon, but he's almost a kid, more her age than her mother's. It turns out his own mother lives in the ground, his words, right next door to the girl's daddy. What a riot, the little Elvis says, all of us being so close together like that. He begins jawboning with the mother, the two of them swaying in rhythm like saplings.

Her daddy's a whole lot nicer now that he's dead. The girl can tell him anything and he listens. His grave still looks fresh, each letter chiseled neatly into the stone, and the grass is clipped. It's like a national park. All the neighbors are quiet and everything, and it's all paid for. The only thing your daddy's benefits covered was final expenses, her mother likes to say, at least *he* gets to rest easy now. Even with her mother chattering to the little Elvis, working him up, the girl can hear herself think here, tell her daddy things, stories he never had time for when he was drinking. He was always more interested in what she felt like under her dress than in what she might have to say. When her mother found out about it—the girl never told, the whole thing was all too complicated—she left him like she did the others and he always told the girl, mostly over the phone, how it dried him up. "I love you both," was the last thing he said. She admits she liked him more when he wasn't around, except for the times he took her to the airport. He was a liar and all like that, but even so, they were kindred spirits.

The little Elvis comes with them for tacos, something the girl thought might happen. All the way to the taco joint, the girl sits in back and listens. Her mother sucks up while they pass through one of those pretty neighborhoods. It depresses the girl, all the houses with their big yards and enough space for a ghost to live in. The little Elvis, retard that he is, finally gets the picture, that her mother thinks he's the real thing and all like that, and his fingers crawl along the backrest. The girl's father used to do the same thing with his fingers on the bed when he came to tell the girl her bedtime story. Next thing the girl knows, those stubby Elvis fingers are massaging her mother's collarbone, but little Elvis is dumb enough to look back at the girl and grin. "What about it, Pork Chop? You want a taco, a big sloppy burritto with all the juice running out?" The little Elvis laughs. The girl rolls her eyes so he can know she thinks he's a dummy. "Take off them glasses, honey," the little Elvis says. "Let me see your eyes real good." The girl stares at him over the plastic frames like one of her two role models, the librarian at the branch library. He grins. "Whatever you want, sugar buns, it's all on me."

"Mama," the girl whines, "tomorrow was my dancing day." She's wearing her only pair of leotards, pulled real fast from a rubber-coated line strung between the trailer and a pockmarked tree.

"Don't worry about it, sweetheart. The whole mystery of a woman's life lies ahead of you. Don't go attaching to some false idol." Her mother honks at a tractor-trailer parked halfway into the two-lane. They're in redneck country again, looking for something swanky, a Chi-Chi's or like that, now that they know the little Elvis is picking up the tab. "Hurricane coming through these parts soon, anyway. Those trailers, they'll be in Mobile Bay. Besides, those library books in the back seat are way overdue. Didn't they come from Jackson? Honey, check the due date on them while you're riding back there, will you do that?"

There's one book, that's all. It's dusty, stained with cola and forty miles of rough road. Same old, same old, the girl thinks, mimicking her dance instructor, her other role model. She teaches kids for free once a week in the high-school gym a mile from the trailer. "There's not even a card in it, Mama. We lost the card." It's a book about organic gardening they keep to compensate for the fact they've never had a garden or even turned a spade. It's one thing, like cooking, her mother refuses to do for any man, even in the very beginning.

Remove all sods, weeds, and existing plants, the girl reads. *Add peat moss, sand, and sheep manure.* There's a lot in the book about perennials, annuals. *Shrubs have large, sprawling root systems and are dangerous to smaller plants.*

The restaurant looks like Mexico. "We're on vacation!" her mother shouts. All the waitresses wear long flowered skirts. One long wall has a painting of an archway and a big hacienda. Everybody's happy, and the girl wonders whether they stay that way once they leave. They order almost everything on the menu, her mother winking the whole time. Little Elvis squints and checks his wallet, but her mother rubs his leg up real good and spits in his ear until he starts smiling. After the tacos and beans and rice and margaritas, plenty of those, he smacks his lips, loudly on purpose to show he liked what he ate. He's got both of them on the same side of the booth with him. "Where we going now, babes?"

Her mother is all lit up. "We going back to that graveyard to ask your mama's permission for some hanky-panky. Lots of nice soft grass in that graveyard. A man can feel right at home there, you get what I mean?" Her devil-smile is plastered across her face. The girl is getting drunk even without much tequila. She's grinning like a nitwit. The retard winks at her, rolls his tongue around in his mouth and slops down the rest of his drink like it's going out of style. He laughs from the gut, and for the first time actually sounds like Elvis, but there's no way the girl thinks he's cute. Then he forgets all about her because he needs both hands on her mother; he's trying to talk her into the motel next door. Her mother shushes him. "I don't leave my daughter in no parking lot," she says. "It's a little different by the graveyard. She can take in some fresh air, study all the stars. It's good for her." She's got him love-whispering by now, speaking to that place between her legs where she likes to say all men dream of going.

"We can leave the little one somewhere nice, sugar pie."

"You'll see how little she is," her mother says. Little Elvis squints again, trying to imagine the possibilities. The girl's mother is grinning her ass off. The poor sucker is nothing but meat. "Someone like you," she says, "you must obtain *assent* from beyond before doing what we gonna do. We gonna bushwhack you, bring you back into the world of flesh and blood."

Outside, it's almost dark. At the cemetery, the little Elvis makes out with the mother a little bit, then stumbles from the car. The girl climbs into the front seat. Then little Elvis gets her mother's door open, tries to pull her out. "Hey, wait a goddamn second," she says. "You talk to your mama first. You get her okay, *then* call us. We'll come running." She's got her hand climbing up his leg. He leans into a sloppy kiss, one hand on a breast. "Give *her* a reason to wait, too," her mother says, motioning to the girl, and he leans across the seat, looks the girl flat in the face. "You the kind of sugar she thinks you is?" he says. The girl smiles an imitation of her mother's devil-smile and licks her lips. He pulls himself to her like a snake and kisses the girl, his crotch wiggling in the mother's lap. He sure don't kiss like a ghost, leaves the girl with her glasses all steamy and the taste of hair cream in her nose.

He stands besides the car, swaying like his skinny snakeskin boots won't hold him up. His eyes are glassy. "How I know you gonna wait?"

"Aw, baby." Her mother takes the key out of the ignition and tucks it in his pants. "How can you doubt?" She waves him away. "You go to your mama. When you give us a yell, we'll come fetch more than that key. We'll see where that key might fit." He swaggers off into the gloom like a sailor at the docks and they wait a minute or so. Then the girl's mother opens her purse and finds the other key. They tear off into the night with a hollar and a whoop. Her mother reaches under her own butt and passes the girl his wallet. "He had two big bulges when he was kissing you, honey, I had to work real good to make sure he put his whole mind on the other one."

The wallet's still warm, and her mother drives so fast, passing so many cars to get them back on the Interstate, that the wallet's about to fly from the girl's hand. It's a little ugly somehow, all sweat-stained with a smell like vinegar, so she opens the glovebox and tosses it in. The girl is getting real creeped out now, a regular *Nightmare on Elm Street,* wondering whether the little Elvis might dig up her daddy to get even.

In the clear, nothing but road, but her mother's still weaving, trying to reach into the glove box. It's not the wallet she wants now, it's a map. "The one from the welcome station, honey," she says. "You know that place those Cree Indians had their setup, told us about that Trail of Tears to Oklahoma they managed to miss?"

The girl climbs into the back seat for the book about gardening. Book in hand, she tries getting her mother interested in the scenery, what there is of it. Trailer parks again, honky-tonks, rusty tractors. No open road, not yet, though interstate signs crop up more frequently, blue-and-white announcements of something different, a new guy for the mother, another sofa bed for the girl. *In Africa,* the girl reads, *white is the color of death; an African violet is a special expression of happiness.*

Her mother decides to splurge, find them a fancy motel, one with a lounge and a pool, but before they get there, wherever there is, her mother remembers a man who played a part-time cop on television and now lives in a swanky suburb. They go way back. The girl is nodding off, lights all around them and street signs getting dizzy. Her dance teacher taught the girl how to spin without falling over, and she tries to focus on a single neon sign, the center of the universe blinking on and off and advertising Buddy Burgers, but it gets all fuzzy. "At least we're not in Birmingham, sugar. Remember that time your daddy worked in the mills for all of three weeks?" The girl mumbles something and starts dreaming her daddy from the grave, a regular *Nightmare on Elm Street* again, and next thing the girl knows they're parked scattershot, the front half of the car on the lawn at a big ranch house, her mother pounding away on a cathedral door, screaming "Henry! Henry!" until the door opens and a good-looking man in a bathrobe scratches his chin and stands in the bright doorway, a kid's tricycle just behind him gleaming. Fireflies are coming on and somebody behind the house is punching nails into pieces of wood with some kind of machine. Whoosh. Whoosh. Whoosh. It sounds like those air guns to scare away birds you can hear at a big airport if you lie on the end of the runway at night while the planes come in, the way the girl and her daddy used to do when he was drunk and wanted to show her a good time. She'd have a big glass of gin on the way to the airport until everything got real fuzzy, then they'd wait for a plane to blast the tops of their heads off.

An electric bug killer keeps snatching fireflies out of the air. Her mother's voice gets loud again until the man puts an arm around her, looking over his shoulder back into the house, which must be full of empty rooms, nothing but furniture and all that, empty beds, a refrigerator with cold milk and leftover apple pie. He's got on one of those big bathrobes like a bear might wear. Her mother's snuggling against it now, but it's real obvious he wants to get rid of them.

The girl looks away from the pitiful scene for a moment to the highway, close enough to see all the cars with their air conditioning full blast going somewhere far away, radios playing Elvis or somebody like that, somebody with a life, a cup of cola keeping their guts cool while they drive along telling each other jokes.

"Come see her, come see my baby," her mother croons, begging, and he comes over to the car, still in his bathrobe. He's giving her mother a bottle of something brown, forcing her to take it. She's trying to insinuate the girl is his, but he won't have none of it. He wasn't born yesterday.

"How you doing, sweetheart?" Some faint music is coming from somewhere. His voice is warm as molasses and the girl can tell he means her no harm. "I remember you from TV," she says. "You played a cowboy and then a cop. You were on 'The Rockford Files' once, huh?"

"You remember that, sweetheart? Bless you." He smiles one of those gone smiles, the kind you hardly see anymore. Her daddy had that kind of smile, sometimes he'd just give it for no reason, didn't want nothing for it, at least not at the time. Just out to have himself a day, not at anybody's expense.

Her mother's still trying to snuggle into the bathrobe like it might fit them both. "You got to go," he says, "I can't have this." He looks back at that open door, big enough to drive a jeep through. "But I wish you all the luck in the world." They get back on the highway, her mother cursing under her breath and crying at the same time.

She's having trouble keeping the car straight while she fiddles with the radio. "Goddamn religious crap! Can't you find nothing else on the dial? Months of grits and burnt toast and that clammy skin I'll never in my life forget and this is it? Can't you find us some blues, some country, some rock-n-roll? You know, honey, like some *rock-n-roll*. Hymns!" The girl knows what her mother is thinking. The last one wanted to drag them both to church on Sunday, after all the things he did in between. "Ever notice how it's hymns and not hers?"

"Mama!"

The blare of a horn, a deep-voiced shout from the other lane, something about women and cars. Her mother has found the map. She straightens out the wheel, looks in the rearview, and gives the finger to the receding taillights before struggling with the map, still driving, foot still hard on the pedal, face scarred with a frown. "That sonofabitch," she says, the asphalt before them forgotten. They swerve to the Interstate, but too fast. They nearly tilt.

They drive all night, the moon blue somewhere in the sky, following them down to the Gulf of Mexico. Every so often they stop for coffee or cups of ice and some Coke. The brown stuff in the bottle disappears and her mother gets so hyper she bounces while she drives, telling the girl the story of her life, but the girl mostly nods off until the sun cracks the windshield. The girl can't believe they went all night, they've never quite done that until now, and in fact the girl sort of remembers stopping somewhere after dreaming of the runway and the planes, sleeping without moving in a parking lot at a rest area.

Her mother's talking too fast, even faster than she did during the night, thinking enough talk might straighten the car if she forgets to turn the wheel at the end of a straightaway. The girl is keeping the car steady, too, leaning to the right when the wheel veers left and vice-a-versa. It would be funny, a cutesy-pie hysterical fit, both of them chaw-chawing, except now the heat's on outside the car, the sun blazing in the front seat. "Mama, you sure you on the right road? I think we're going back the way we came." Her mother laughs, her devil-smile too scary to look at, her forehead dripping sweat, dark mascara caked in the corners of her eyes. Both of them go for their visors, their dark glasses. The car's so old there's nothing above its windshield anymore to come down and keep the sun out. The girl smells the smell of hot vinyl and sweat, like the sound her bladder makes when it's full, and it is, but she doesn't ask her mother to stop, not yet, because she won't. It takes a dozen lights or fifty highway miles to earn one gas station.

Her mother fiddles with the radio some more. "What you say to some burritos?" she shouts. "What you say to some frijoles, some honky-tonk burritos, an all-day drive to Houston?"

They stop instead for fast-food tacos, get lost looking for cheap gas, somehow end up with bladders empty and the sun still smackdab in their faces, but the time nowhere near midday, not unless time got turned all inside out when the girl was nodding off. Anything is possible.

"Mama, you know what I think? You been making circles while I was zonked."

"Goddamn, that's not possible," she says under her breath. "You better not be right about that." She's pissed at the girl now for bringing up the obvious, but she's talking to herself, all under her breath, and you know there's something wrong when she does that. Her hair is all tangled from the wind and the all-night drive and the girl gathers from this talk her mother is giving herself, a real lecture by now, that she knows how drunk and tired and fucked-up she is. "Honey, I got to get some sleep." Her mother eyes the median, and then they both see the sign for Tuscaloosa. "What the hell is this? A time warp? Let's just switcheroo to the other side."

"Mama, no," the girl whispers, her glasses already flying from her face, toward a puddle on the median. "We'll flip." There's nothing but grass to look at, nothing but windshield between the girl and wet grass, but a few minutes later, speeding the other way to make up for lost time, the sun a little behind them but gaining, they spot the little Elvis, hitching no doubt to New Orleans, his black velvet pants all spangled with little stars, epaulets on the shoulders of his Nashville shirt. His eyes bug out of his head and he waves frantically, starts hollaring after them. The girl grabs the wallet from the glove box and tosses it out the window. "What the hell you do that for?" Her mother's shouting her ass off, the car tilting this way and that, the wind screaming in the window. "We should pick him up!"

"Mama, he'll kill us! You stole his wallet and left him at that graveyard with his mama!"

"Shit, honey, he ain't at the graveyard no more. That's Elvis! You just a little blind without your glasses. He hitches these highways all the time, tells us what it's like to live with Jesus, then just disappears, goes back to his mama. I think he's a little lonely these days, honey, and horny as hell, a little like Jesus. He could go off and be happy somewhere all by his lonesome, but he wants to give us the good news. You know what I mean? When he died, some people saw him in the clouds, waving, carrying on, promising not to leave us. He's back, sweetheart. Don't doubt that for a minute."

She goes on like that, still drunk or just crazy with the road, dreaming about the little Elvis, while the girl mourns for her glasses, back in the puddle on the median, not good to a soul. She misses them more than her daddy, but missing them that way gets her thinking again about him. On the radio, some preacher is strutting down that sawdust trail, just him and Jesus. He wants to save their souls, plunge them into the body of Christ, sail with them to Jerusalem, bottle the mud from the grave of Jesus, heal their wallets so they can grow and prosper, but it's not Sunday yet, it's just Alabama, and if Elvis can come back, so can her daddy. *If you place him in the hole roots down, grasp his trunk about halfway up and shake him vigorously from side to side,* to get all the air out, he'll leave the graveyard in his best suit, make his way to the airport, his wingtip shoes spic-and-span even in the dust, and lie down drunk when it gets dark on the runway.

All the planes that land and take off go right through him, all those landing lights twinkle like Christmas, and he stretches out his arms, screaming, the top of his head coming off to the sound of jet engines, the same kind of screaming sound a car engine will make from inside when it finally turns upside down and the motor won't switch off.

Waiting for Ruth

Birth, growth, existence, reproduction, decay, vanishing," Gilbert intoned, able to think of nothing else, even though it wasn't quite accurate—Ruth never reproduced. The black and dark greens stiffly repeated the words, glancing at each other. They must be as contemptuous of me as I am of them, Gilbert thought, though at least they understand the necessity of ritual. He slid the memorial stone into its resting place near the beach. His fingernails scratched across polished marble with a sound like the tines of a fork on a blackboard.

Sidney, meanwhile, sat on Ruth's towel at the beach in his bluestriped trunks, in sight of the place where she drowned, caught in the undertow. If the words resonated at all across waves of heat, they traveled like metallic whispers through air, through stillness, traveled like electricity in wires. Wearing a pair of mirrored sunglasses, Sidney stared across white sand. They were all playing some obscure game, like the rescue squads a few days earlier, when the sand was cluttered with figures. Bystanders, police, diving teams, all with their frayed paraphernalia of hope. Low-flying planes glinted near the waves.

Sidney's mother had an urn to take home and keep on her mantel for Sidney. The urn was Gilbert's idea, something tangible to hold on to and let go of. He'd even found some ashes to put inside it. Instead of accepting it with grace and decorum, she had swooned into his arms. Heat stroke, he feared, holding his breath against musky perfume, but she revived quickly, even managed to walk from the beach with the others. "What can we do for Sid?" they wanted to know, curious or sympathetic or appalled, as comic in their formal unanimity as a party of penguins waddling off into the sunset.

"I'll take care of it," Gilbert told them, glad to see them go. Better if they returned to their social habitats, where they wouldn't have to think about the indifference of wind and waves. As for Gilbert, he would nurse a drink in his summer house, white curtains rustling, then jog for miles, feeling only his heartbeat, sea breezes, his body vital, sturdy.

Sidney didn't believe in Ruth's death. Only a few hours before, adjusting collars or ties, many of his neighbors had received him. "This service is inappropriate because Ruth isn't dead," he told them. Joyce Rusk took what he was saying for grief and offered condolences. He stared at her. "If you're crazy enough to think she's dead, you can go to hell." One or two of the others, like Pat and John Eliot, well-versed in the nuances of shock, told him to buckle up, old man, face facts. That sort of thing. Instead, he lost his temper. Gilbert could hardly picture Sid lifting a cane chair, much less tossing it through a window, but the story traveled too fast to change much in the telling.

Once they all vanished through the heat, their dark torsos sliding off their legs and tumbling down a curve of beach, Gilbert turned to face the memorial plaque, hypnotizing himself with the ceaseless crash and cradlerock of ocean.

*

"Hello, Sid." Gilbert startled him, his approach shielded by the beach house. Compulsively Sidney rearranged Ruth's towel, placed a hand firmly on the binoculars beside him, and stared out to sea. A single gull slanted through the sun. In his dark glasses Gilbert saw his own reflection, and felt he was falling, uncertain where he might land. "The service is over," he said. "If you like, you can have dinner at my place. You can rest."

"I can't leave the beach."

"Look, Sid, she's gone. If you'd stood over there with the rest of us, you'd be closer to the bone of that thought by now. We all loved her, but starving yourself or pretending nothing's happened won't help. We miss her, too, but we're worried about you. Come with me."

"She's not dead. In fact, I saw her last night. If she were dead, we would have her body. The body would wash ashore."

"Sid, there's nothing out there." So many times Gil had reasonably thought through an impasse, suggesting compromise, calming tempers. "Look, this is absurd, you're tired. Why don't we walk a couple miles, have a drink? That'll help you sleep." Gilbert himself was well-versed in the nuances of insomnia. "You can't just sit here." Sidney picked up the binoculars and studied the horizon. Gilbert shrugged and walked to the beach road, past the blare of a boombox. When he looked back, Sidney's binoculars were still trained on the swooping gull, sweeping or hovering in rhythm with its wheeling flight.

✳

"He can stay here," his mother said. "He belongs here." Fully recovered from her faint, she talked Gilbert drowsy. A floor fan oscillated behind her, its mechanical breeze giving new life to a dying fern, its noise and the drone of her voice hypnotizing him. For some time now, Sidney had lived in an isolated cottage with Ruth and with Stephanie, his sister, but in his mother's presence he became patronizing or very subdued: his sense of himself visibly shrank. Perhaps he was better off at the beach. With his identity undermined, Gilbert thought, she might easily convince him to stay, a genteel mother-and-son living together in a throwback to an earlier age, sharing a surname which may not have been aboard the Mayflower but which still carried its social weight.

Photographs of Sidney covered the walls. A slender child with a sand bucket, easily given to colds; a full-faced adolescent in a prom outfit, posed with his sister because he was too shy to ask anyone else for a date; a bearded emaciated face, framed by a cap and gown and a Princeton diploma which did nothing to improve his lack of inner equilibrium; a lost soul in trunks on the beach, taking a year to travel and search for the past his bashfulness had taken from him. "He'll forget, as they say. I mean, that's what he has to do, isn't it, dear?"

The chair Gilbert sat in had thick upholstery. He stroked it and stared at post cards, stuffed owls, cigarette holders from Europe, ceramic animals. For a certain sort of old woman, time doesn't pass, people don't change. When Sidney first introduced Ruth, his salvation, his soul-companion, to his mother, the grand introduction, Ruth had a cold. She suffered through an agony of icy solicitude: cough medicines, aspirin, bitter tea, a bolster for her head.

"Perhaps it's better," Gilbert suggested, fondling a small ceramic elephant, "if Sid stays at the cottage with Stephanie. Maybe that will help him come to terms with what's happened." At that first meeting, Ruth in fact glowed with vitality, and finally rose from the davenport for a "tour." She and Gilbert exchanged wry smiles that Sidney was too nervous to appreciate or even notice.

"Really? You think so? He'll remember everything there." She thinks I'm an ally, Gilbert thought, interested in connections, someone who knows his place, who has no credentials except her son's friendship and my unofficial role in the summer as village troubleshooter.

"It's not really for us to decide, is it?" Through the window over her shoulder he saw Sidney, still in blue trunks, step to the porch. The screen door slammed. His mother started.

"Hello, everybody," he said. His mother, ready to return him to the sanctuary of the past she imagined he once lived in, started to rise, arms opening. He placed a hand on her shoulder. "No, don't get up, not for me. Don't disturb yourself. I can't stay."

"Darling, let me fix you something to eat." The bottom of her face was slack.

"That would be nice," he said. Still, he held her down. "Maybe some other time? I'm just here to pick something up." He hurried into the bedroom. Unable to contain herself, she followed.

Gilbert sat alone as a shower of late-afternoon sun puddled on the floor.

Sidney emerged with a sleeping-bag under one arm.

"Delinquents, beach bums, stray dogs, and worse," his mother said. He answered politely, his voice soothing, and Gilbert, standing restlessly now, opened the screen door for him.

"You know where Ruth is, don't you?" Sidney asked. His glance dissected Gilbert. Until Gilbert emptied his mind and took a cleansing breath, as though jogging, a flurry of associations careened wildly through his mind, a canoe adrift in white-water. She's lost, elsewhere, I don't know, he thought, but yes, dead, accept loss or become its victim. "You *do* know where she is." Sidney's voice was blotchy, beginning to peel. He still wore the blue-striped trunks. "I tell you what. If she should by chance end up at your place, will you tell her I'm waiting?"

*

Ruth appeared that night. A shower pelted the roof until morning. Unable to sleep, Gilbert jogged through rain, the cool splash of water, the churning of ocean against its shores, the sound of bare feet on wet sand. Everything felt right. He had routines, and they were harmonious with the cruel traction of the world.

Back in bed, damp towel around his waist, insomnia lifted; he drifted between cool pelting rain on the roof and more rapid waters of nightmare where Ruth swam, liquid, whirling. The sun splashed a rainstorm of light, soaking her hair, drenching her with sun and shadow, body towed helplessly, lungs full of water, arms aflail.

On the beach road next morning he met Stephanie, walking barefoot, avoiding bits of gravel and swords of beach grass, hair braided and curled into a knot, as though grief required a mourning-cap. "Going to check on Sid," she said.

"I'll come along. I want to retrieve those Melvilles Ruth borrowed."

Bleary-eyed, Sidney refused to leave the beach until Stephanie agreed to take his place. Eyebrow screwed up, he stared at Gilbert. "You going to wait?"

"Not for Ruth, no." Sidney smiled sardonically and stumbled away. In the dry slanting glare of morning, he was clearly mad. Gilbert told Stephanie her indulgence fed into his delusion and became outright participation in his madness.

"Get off it. I spend part of my day on the beach, why not now?" Handfuls of scooped sand trickled through long fingers. "Whatever made you think up that charade on the beach? It was grotesque, that plaque, those people."

Gilbert pulled his brows close, hooding his eyes. "People die. What would you have us do? Pretend she stepped out for a pack of cigarettes?" With a wave of her hand, Stephanie contemptuously dismissed the routines of community life—a special ordinance that allows a section of isolated beach to serve as a memorial, the muted punctuation of a funeral, a solid line of type in the obituary columns. Independent, talented, a young painter who knew her craft and didn't imitate the latest rage, thick highways of paint scraped across the canvas with a rake, she still refused to be serious, never worked for a living. That's what Gilbert thought. People looked out for her. Gilbert was one of them.

"I don't believe in funerals because I've been there," she said, refusing to face him. "Things fall into place." For a moment he wondered whether she was taking her promise to Sidney seriously. A nervous leap of her eyes usually qualified or deepened her words; a twist of her full mouth hinted at her mood. But now he had only a severe angular profile of a dark woman sitting cross-legged, staring at coins of sunlight on the water. "Artificial bouquets, business suits, who needs it? Besides, most of those creeps were there to make you feel better, not because they thought a few poems and speeches on a beach was a great idea." She sifted another handful of sand. "You ever see one of those New Orleans funerals with a brass band? That sort of thing would be okay." She trailed off. "I like to imagine her far out at sea. I like to think she's halfway to Africa by now."

Gilbert touched her. She stiffened. "No. I don't need your solicitude."

"Even your mother knows the value of ritual." He chose his words carefully. "She protects investments, avoids exploitation."

"I still burn candles for my father. Burning candles isn't a ritual?" She turned to him.

He was lost, swimming in dark eyes. "I dreamed of Ruth last night, that couldn't have happened by itself. The memorial service had to snap something into place. Ritual. Ritual helps. Ritual, exercise."

"Exercise?" She looked thunderstruck, a hand raised to one cheek.

"Activity. He needs to survive, that's the first priority."

"God, you're a mushbrain. You're not even you. You're a pod that looks like you. Is that it?" She drew in her lips. "All that Hemingway crap, that Bogart stuff. A stiff drink, a pull on a cigarette?" She covered her thighs completely with sand. "Ever think Sid might need something besides three rounds in the ring?"

"*You* can wait if you like," he said, standing and stretching in his sweats. "I've got a date with some saw grass."

He slapped through sand, light surf, past an occasional sunbather, relishing the thought of the estuary and its breezes, concentrating on his breath, but still Ruth rose, disappearing in the undertow, arms waving, a corner of her mouth twisted because he wasn't there to save her.

✳

Heavy-limbed, torpid, strangely ill at ease, he nursed a drink as daylight faded. He was stupified, unable to move, his bones dusty, filtered through lamplight and the pages of a book.

He woke, book still in hand, to the screen door banging on its hinges, curtains blowing wildly. Again he had dreamed of Ruth, in a gallery, a portrait museum. Ruth, Sidney, and Gilbert. A screen of moss or gray hair covers every picture. Portraits of Gandhi, Einstein, Lou Gehrig—dozens of paintings and photographs, all slowly breathing. Ruth covers her face with a pair of claws, bends over, the claws mutate into shovels. She tunnels into the sand-floor of the gallery. Sidney calls after her, the sand is serene, undisturbed. They're alone in a vast desert, Gilbert takes a portrait in his hands, a small cameo.

He latched the door and window. The phone rang. "Is Sid there?" Stephanie asked.

"No. Something wrong?"

"Yes. No. I don't know, okay?"

Light-headed, far from his stupor, he couldn't touch ground. "What do you mean?"

"You don't know what I mean? Well, let me tell you, okay? Is that all right?" He could see her eyes, leaping with each phrase. "What's wrong, he wants to know."

Someone knocked viciously on the screen door and kicked its bottom panel. "Let me in!" Sidney shouted. He pulled on the door, moved to the window.

"Listen, okay? After all this, let's celebrate. Okay? Celebrate. No funeral, a celebration. Get it?" As Gilbert put down the phone, Sidney smashed the window with an old board, stepped through shards of glass and splinters of wood, and shook his head, wild-eyed. "Hello," he said, and plucked small splinters from his skin. His eyes darted into the dark bedroom. "How are you? A tad chilly?"

He was bleeding. "You want a towel?" Gilbert tried to be gentle, but he wasn't practiced at it. Still, aggravated impatience was clearly no way to handle a weak man in the middle of breakdown.

"Oh, that." He glanced at the curtains. "I'm sorry. I lost my balance. But I'll replace it."

"It's just a window, Sid. That's not the problem. You're the problem. If you're not part of the solution, you're part of the problem. Don't try to pretend nothing's changed. Everything's changed."

"You don't mind if I take a leak." He sauntered from room to room, searched cabinets, opened garbage cans and closet doors, flushed the toilet and returned, still blood-spotted. "You think I don't know what's going on?" He leaned against the wall.

"Nothing's going on, Sid."

"Last night I dreamed of rising," he said. "I was on my back on a mattress in a white room with white furniture. Wicker, I think. There were lots of people, mostly strangers. They were urging me to fly. So I tried. I floated up. The sky was white, too. It was nice, very peaceful."

If only Gilbert could take him to a gravesite, dig up her body, grab him by the scruff of the neck, tell him to see. Look at this, Sid. Look. He struggled for composure and smiled.

"I have to go," Sidney said. "Ruth's coming home tonight." He screwed up his eyebrow. "I want to be there."

He tripped off the porch into the night.

The heart knows its ways, they tell me, but I've never seen much proof, Gilbert thought. He was anxious to call Stephanie, to convince her to put him away for a little while, shoot him up or hypnotize him until he came back to the world, but first he poured a stiff drink and broiled a steak. He ate it carefully, slowly, savoring each bite. Then he cleaned up the debris and tacked a strip of cloth over the broken window.

"He's in great shape," he told Stephanie on the phone. "Jumped through the window, searched the place and went home to meet her. Is he back yet?"

"I don't know. I mean, I'm staying with friends. He wanted the place to himself. He's all right?"

"Look, he needs attention. Convince him to get it. He's having a breakdown. It happens, to some people. Nothing to be ashamed of."

"Look, spare the sermon. You afraid?"

"What do you mean, afraid?"

"He's jealous, he might jump you. It scares you, I understand that."

"Jesus Christ."

"Have you thought jealousy might be good for him?"

Ruth had the ability to mediate between opposites. She protected Sid, provided him with a word or two, a glance to shift his bearings, reach a new awareness. Maybe Stephanie expected that to happen. But without Ruth it was impossible, and his emotional outbursts insulted them all, Gilbert felt. Get flighty or fanciful and you're lost.

He reached the cottage in twenty minutes. Through its small porch window a table lamp glowed near the sofa. Gilbert couldn't quite make out the words, but he heard Sidney talking to someone, so he knocked and called out to him, to save him. The door opened, Sidney smiled. "Come in." He tilted up one eye. "You can't take her away, you know." He hunched before Gilbert. "Sit on the sofa," he said, working his knuckles. "The rest of our place is off-limits."

"Off-limits? What are you hiding, Sid, an inflatable doll?" The living room, Stephanie's room, was filled with ferns. The shadows of ferns flickered on walls, windowsills, the ceiling. Sid karate-chopped his palms in menacing fashion, balanced on the balls of his feet, swaying, involved in some intricate dance.

"You're trying to take her away, aren't you? Leave me with nothing."

"I gave her to you. Why would I want her back?"

Sidney karate-chopped Gilbert harmlessly in the chest. They embraced, grappled like wrestlers in dim light and huge rolling shadows of ferns. Gilbert quickly worked his way behind him, an old service trick, and tripped him up. Sidney was stronger than Gilbert thought, but even at the start his muscles trembled, and Gilbert pushed him to the sofa with a muffled sound. He felt dizzy, standing over Sidney, uncertain who controlled the situation. Sidney turned to his back and stared at the white, empty ceiling. "Sid?"

"Haven't you done enough?" Stephanie's doorway voice startled Gilbert, who jumped as if bitten and turned. "How long you been there?"

She stared at him, still hunched for an attack.

"We better call an ambulance," he said, straightening.

"Yes, that's true. Please go away. Okay?"

They sat in silence among ferns, Sidney vacant-eyed on the couch, Stephanie stroking his forehead. When the village ambulance arrived, Gilbert left. On the beach, hands in pocket, he listened to the ocean and trailed sand until morning. The world took on the mood of a dream. The wind on his cheeks, the daily commerce between common sense and mystery, so easy to sink into forever, so self-indulgent. Grains of sand between his toes whirled into orbit, he stumbled home drunk with insomnia to sit near the window Sid tumbled through. A gull dropped from the morning sun, wings on fire, face wrinkled and human, spotted with newborn blood. The hypnotic pattern of shadows swirled like curtains, splashes, long dizzy falls. His phone was an unanswered cry from another world, the endless horizon of possible human contact so terrifying he ran great distances, ate well to survive whatever was happening, to fix on the cruelty of the world, and find purchase on the solid earth. There's nothing else, above or below, he thought sternly. Ruth, Sidney, Stephanie took on the wavering forms of figures seen in lightning and rain, Ruth before him in early light, hair soaked, Stephanie at the door, eyes staring, but the doorway was empty. When he heard Sidney had recovered

69

and was living with his mother, the life she wanted after all, it was time for Gilbert to leave. He decided to walk to see Sidney, say farewell to whatever remained of their friendship, punctuate the summer, but on the beach he stopped, wet sand between his toes. He couldn't go on. He stared at the ocean, his toes, fingers, the light springy hairs on the back of one hand. Who was he? What was this stuff?

Only breath and the body matters, he told himself, discipline. What else is there? What else can there be besides the will except for soft sinking marshland and the bottomless stories of the ocean where everyone drowns without beginning or end? Think of the body, he demanded of himself, but at Stephanie's cabin, where he walked without knowing it, he was breathing hard, not right with the world.

He was alone, too grievously alone for any theory to make sense.

The door opened, Stephanie stepped to the porch. With her hair pulled back, she looked something like Ruth, Gilbert thought. "Hello. You want that set of books?"

"No."

"Well. What then?" She turned from him to face the dunes, with their driftwood, their tides, their winds perpetually funneling at a slant into the earth, their sentimental sand castles that washed away each morning, their black moonlit waves that glinted bright in the sun like grain to be walked on and harvested. "Cat got your tongue?" she said. Then she turned to face him and he felt as though he was losing himself in her stare. Neither blinked, and for just a moment the crash and cradlerock of surf rose to meet them both, and they listened together to the watery compass of time.

INCOMING ROUNDS

I.

The plant conservatory outside the gates of the Lincoln Park Zoo in Chicago was glassy-green and moldy, as alien to the highrises west of the park as a pagan temple. Inside, in hot air full of moist, clinging things, Lydia stared at the unwrinkled stillness of a small pond. Stubbled buildings, she thought, a phrase from some waking dream. She was pregnant not with child but with fat lopsided fears. Stubbled buildings, muggers, shave them all away. They could be anywhere, on the lakefront, behind newspapers, over chessboards, could stroll to her daughter Robin's school, put out their cigarettes and eat the child right up, make her disappear to the size of a grainy photograph taped to a light post. She would be too frightened to scream.

Her husband Bruce, in a waist-length Army jacket and aviator shades, was sermonizing the plants in a rapid-fire voice. "Owning a gun is a form of Buddhism," he said, scratching the three-day growth on his face. "The vets who became Buddhists were the best killers, better than Special Forces." Ahead, Robin disappeared into a roomful of ferns. "Guns and Buddhism," Lydia said, manic with caffeine. "This is wonderful. Why don't you talk about Mars? Why don't you say the moon is green?" She shook dollops of humidity from her forehead. "Why don't you just leave now instead of next week?"

"You're taking this wrong, Lydia. Some time apart will do us good. I'll study murals, learn graffiti, do some writing. We can both breathe." Bruce was gathering material for a book on WPA murals and public street art in Chicago and New York.

"You jerk. You just want an easy way out."

He stopped in his tracks. "That's your trick, babe," he said, and crouched over an untied shoestring. "You're the one who thinks anything more risky than living inside a paperweight is the dungeon, but I don't take the easy way out. No sir, not me. Time enough in the grave for that." Under the force of his anger, Lydia covered her face below the eyes with one hand, as though donning a surgical mask. "That's it," she mumbled, "snap your fingers, change your mind."

Robin sauntered up, a sword-like leaf in her hand, and stood over Bruce, still fumbling with the shoestring. "Stop fighting, I'm back." She pricked him playfully in the face. "What's wrong, Bruce, can't tie your shoe?"

"Cut it out," he said. He grabbed her wrist and pretended to tickle her. "The tickle-beast! He's here!"

"How immature." Robin frowned. "You want me to call the cops? This is abuse, buster. One scream and they'll lock you up, maybe for good. You know about inappropriate touching?"

Bruce raised his hands as though under arrest. "Hey hey hey/Aren't we precocious today," he chanted. "You win, high and mighty. You loved that tickle-beast once. But now Ms High and Mighty, just like your mother." Lydia refused to fly off the handle. She sat on a bench half-obscured by ferns. *The choices we make,* one of her clients had said. "Maybe you've had a stroke," she told Bruce, "maybe that's why you're like this lately," but he wasn't listening anymore. He had a knack for remembering details from the Vietnam era with clairvoyant precision, but otherwise going off into a fugue state or a mystical rhapsody until he didn't know where he was, much less who he was. "Besides," she said, "what would be so bad about living inside a glass paperweight? Lots of snow, a gingerbread cottage, everybody safe, and we could still look around." *A real life that's far more real than what I want,* said the low-pitched voice of another client, a short, stocky Norwegian woman. For nearly a year Bruce once rented an

AP wire-service ticker so he wouldn't miss any news about Vietnam. Every evening he'd settle into a beanbag chair with his headphones, a scissors, and reams of paper, all the day's news. He'd cut-and-paste until midnight. Before he lost interest in the whole endeavor, he filled up four sets of neck-high filing cabinets with clippings and nearly drove Lydia crazy, the machine spitting out fifty words a minute day and night. *You go on for the sake of others. Life is sacrifice.* Her auditory hallucinations intensified. *Sovereign solitude/ In the nude.* "Live inside a paperweight and you meet the witch. Street art, though, that's a different ticket," he said, justifying his new obsession. "Live on the street and you understand lots of things, everything from AIDS to aliens, from Buddha to Jesus. The world is a circle and we're back to square one, babe."

Jesus Christ, she thought, where is my life? *You're abandoned for what you are, not for the role you play.* Where is my life? What have I done with my life?

✳

"NASCAR driving, baby," Bruce said, finally swerving to their curb. "This is a pit stop." Inside, Robin started humming "Yellow Submarine" and Lydia kicked off her shoes. "Parachute to safety," Bruce shouted. He dropped his knapsack near the door. Lydia flopped into the love seat by the bay window. Someone else is inhabiting my body, she thought, someone I should know, and then slipped into her own fugue state, imagining a tumor, maybe in her lungs, maybe inside her heart. There was cancer everywhere and everyone was getting it. "I'm cutting loose," Bruce screamed into her ear, as though it were a walkie-talkie. "I'm hitting the turf on the run. Charlie's a rice field away. Give me air cover, gunships. Dust off! Sucking chest wounds, pelvic bones shattered, legs blown off at the hips!" He grabbed Lydia and pulled her to her feet. "I'll save you, Li-dee-a! Incoming rounds! Incoming rounds! Keep your head down, sweetheart!"

✳

"Why did you give me the name of a bird?" asked Robin at breakfast. "It sounds twerpy."

"That's why," said Bruce.

"Bruce," said Robin. "No teasing, or I'll hide your teeth." She turned a mischievous moon-face to her mother. "Guess who forgot the garbage?"

Lydia studied her bowl of cream of wheat and narrowed her lips. "Sorry," she said sarcastically to Bruce, who smiled. In her husband's dream-time, a house without garbage was unnatural. "Why not compost it?" he said. "Compost it?" she repeated. "Where, for goodness sakes? This is an apartment." Bruce clicked his tongue and snickered. "Well, forget it, then, let the world go to hell. Besides, it's not my place to remember the garbage." Lydia crunched her toast, comparing her life to an Australian aborigine's on a walkabout, something always dangerous around the corner. Downtown, she might walk through somebody's cough and contract TB. The stuff was everywhere.

Robin, reading the back of the cereal box, giggled. Bruce figured out the movies, following the blips with his finger. "At 1:30 it's *Death and the Maiden*. Jimmy Stewart defends a woman accused of shooting her family. I think I'll watch that. At 3:00 it's *Mr. and Mrs. BoJo Jones*. Two teens forced into marriage by pregnancy. Bad news, real bad news." He summarized 'Ryan's Hope,' his favorite soap. "So Ken decided to postpone his suicide until Barry recovered from Faith's affair. And in 'Guiding Light,' Lucille tried to kill Jennifer but stabbed herself instead. Jennifer told the cops it was an accident, because she doesn't want people to know about her *other* identity as Jane Marie. And because she cares for Amanda. She wants to protect her. But on the way to the hospital, Lucille told Amanda Jennifer tried to kill *her* and— "

"Her? Who's *her*?" Robin said. "Amanda or Lucille?"

"Forget it. You're just laughing. No appreciation for the better things in life," Bruce said, grimacing in mock-anger. Robin gripped the breakfast table to keep from falling backwards, her giggles turning into deliberate, antagonizing horselaughs. "Of course I'm laughing, but not at you. At that awful crap. When did you ever get so sensitive?"

"Robin, watch your language," Lydia said.

"Maybe I won't go to New York," Bruce said. "Maybe I'll just lock us all away here until we suffocate or strangle each other. Maybe I'll throw you in the oven." "Don't call me Robin, Bruce. I want another name." Lydia remembered Bruce fiddling with his tie, tugging on it like a noose, arguing, over drinks, that Robin should call her family by their first names. "It's a necessity of modern parenting, Lydia." "Do we even have one opinion in common?" Lydia countered. " 'Momma' or 'Mommy.' Maybe 'Mother.' That's it." That wasn't it. "Mommy is Lydia, Daddy is Bruce, and Grandma is Claire. Who's the baby?" he repeated at dusk a few days later on the lakefront. His fatigue jacket flapping, he tossed Robin in the air.

"The baby is, Lydia!" Robin had shouted. "No, Mommy! No, Daddy!"

✳

"Two hundred thousand years. Remember that," one of her clients said the next day. It was the amount of time it took radioactive waste to decompose to a safe level. Lydia stabbed her notepad with her pen. She worked for a foundation with a grant to find out whether monogamy has a future. With a narrow oily face and ears flush against his head as though greased back with Vitalis, her client talked about nothing but radioactivity, cancer, and corporate criminals. "Are there any other kind?" he mumbled on the way out.

After the interview, overcome by fall fever, she arranged a long lunch break, caught the bus to the zoo, and hurried to the small mammal house, her favorite refuge. Special lighting and sound-proof cubicles tricked furry animals into uncharacteristic daylight activity. She could enter moonlit lives oblivious to her trances. In semidarkness the three-banded armadillo, the bush baby, and the sugar glider would go about their nocturnal affairs. She could drift, let the past possess her, sit outside on a bench and write letters she would never mail. I won't pretend to be someone I'm not, she would vow. I won't see myself in too many eyes. But she also might slip into a trance and imagine the glass paperweight falling to the floor and breaking. Snow everywhere.

75

The building was closed. *To replase brokun glas,* read the sign. The wind was still high, though, and the day as sweet-scented as cinnamon. Winter seemed impossible. Groups of children in bright ski sweaters were chattering. Small mammals on field trips, Lydia thought, walking to the conservatory, where workmen were putting the finishing touches on a pine-scented Christmas display, a world of artificial snow and filtered light. This Christmas, she promised, we'll decorate a big tree. Silver tinsel, frosted snowy lights. We can eat ourselves silly and figure out the movies together.

Giant dinosaur fern. A minute later, in the hot-house stuffiness of the tropical room, she stroked the full-lipped leaves of a rubber plant. Bruce doesn't want to stay, but he doesn't want to give me up. *Tongue fern.* She shook her head, flicking away sweat, nauseated by her insight. This can't be happening, she thought. *Curtain fern.* There must be some way to make it all stop. Claustrophobia wrapped itself around her like a vine; she rushed from the green-stained dome to the curb. She wasn't certain the oncoming bus would stop for her, but it did. Once inside, she fished out some change. The scowling driver, slumped low in his seat, eyes bloodshot, jerked the bus forward, slapping her against the coinbox.

✳

Before Bruce left, he helped her move their things south to her mother's house in Hyde Park. "Without me around," he said, "you'll be safe as a rock. Ice cream every night while I'm slaving away on the mad, gone streets." Then, with a backpack full of clothes and a small suitcase of books and notes, he hoisted Robin, smooched Lydia and left, insisting against her wishes that he could hump it to the train. Alone, she continued the late-night walks they had taken together. Whistle clutched in sweaty fingers, she asserted her right to exist, refusing to heed her mother's warnings. Why should she change her habits simply because she was terrified? She never walked far, maybe down the block to the Medici for a coffee or to the I.C. underpass. Its faded mural, barely visible in the dark, dared her to walk along the viaduct, the way she had done all over the city with Bruce, to another mural on the ghetto side of the University of

Chicago campus. "You ever hear of the phoenix, Lyd?" Bruce would say. "That's what these murals are. You ever hear of *The Wall of Dignity?* We've got to publicize that stuff so it can rise from the ashes." In Hyde Park, they'd leave Robin with her mother and walk from *Alewives and Mercury Fish* on 55th to *Rebirth* on 60th. Bruce vowed more than once that he wanted a wife as devoted to the search for truth and social justice as he was. She took such vows as threats and forced herself to accompany him, no matter what the neighborhood was like, no matter the hour.

Her lakefront walks in the city near her office and the museums took her away from the pressure of people, of storefront displays, the pressure to buy something, eat something, say something to an occasional passing acquaintance. Her restricted evening walks also turned her inward. How cozy it might be to live alone again, she would think, have a flower and a bowl of fruit for company, lock the door and pretend nobody's home when the phone rings.

✳

"Lydia," Robin said at breakfast, "you're not paying attention."

"Yes, I am. You were telling about your painting. About the dog that isn't there." Lydia smiled. "Picture of the Missing Dog."

2.

Lydia was hungry enough to take a bite from the steering wheel but too frightened to park more than a block from the restaurant where she was to meet her friend Natasha, a familiar face from as far back as high school, and another woman. "A consciousness-raising event," Natasha had said. "We'll get drunk and eat whatever we want." It took Lydia almost half an hour to find a parking space; the Near North was full of creeps. Just last month, some girl from the Bible school was raped and stuffed in an alley dumpster behind Second City. Jim Belushi on stage, impersonating a pervert, and that poor girl only a hundred yards away. Even the wrong kind of glance or an unintended nudge on a well-lit corner could be lethal. Hadn't she read that every third person on the Chicago streets carried a gun?

Bruce would have stopped anywhere and hunched over like a grunt, oblivious to shadows, slapping the pocket where he carried a small spray can of drugstore burglar repellent. "Vietnam, Lyd. It's all the Nam." But Lydia stared exhausted into the glassy tabletop, ignoring the conversation, remembering a large sunlit calliope under oak trees she and Bruce rode on together somewhere. Where had they been, New Orleans on vacation, Milwaukee in search of graffiti?

Full of the jargon of a recent transformation to New Age connoisseur, Natasha was in constant motion, her black page-boy hair flipping about and her dark button eyes gleaming translucently as she quickly studied almost everyone in the restaurant. Hanging ferns swung cozy above her head in nets of macrame. The lake was wet in the moonlight, Lydia thought, and frowned. Does that make any sense?

Rock music pounded into her forehead. Her internal word-buzz made response impossible. *Always under surveillance,* some half-conscious voice whispered. "Isn't it nifty," said Natasha, "for women to get together and astral-project?" "Yes, that's certainly *nifty,*" said Pam, a thin bony woman with narrow lips. Natasha's cheeks colored; her eyes lighted on Lydia, then skimmed an exhibit of photos hung above each booth. The snapshots were fashionably scrawled with dark crayon and heavy pencil. "We've got to create ourselves by *talking,*" Pam said. "Language isn't a structure of ideas or regulations to be followed. One thing doesn't have to lead to another. We've got to stand outside our condition and say what needs to be said." "What I'd like to do," Lydia replied, "is put everybody in a comfortable box, with cotton and newspaper, and keep the boxes in a safe fireproof place."

Pam pursed her lips, an eyebrow cocked to hold back a sardonic thin-faced reply. "I know a place that can do that for you," she finally said, leaning a little forward, her voice measured. "It's called a mausoleum." Stopping twice to flirt, a waitress swung her wraparound red skirt like a dancer, deftly avoiding a hand that yearned for her waist, and sashayed to the table with more wine. Lydia stared at her dessert spoon, irritation crawling into her forehead and nestling there, pinching the place where Natasha said everyone had a third eye. Her whole life sounded absurd, like one of her mother's movies or small talk about Rush Week and European summers at the only college ball she ever attended, all the girls dressed in gold or silver strapless formals, their bustlines tinted by shadows and soft lights. Lydia had walked away from her date. At her apartment she had plunged into jeans and listened to Mahler all evening, so intimidated and outraged by the ball and each perfectly-placed kiss curl or corsage that she was barely able to be civil and apologize the next day to her date. I could be one of Bruce's soap operas, she thought. Botched marriage, wretched job, phone calls to New York.

✳

"Muhammed Ali got beat," Bruce said on the phone. "Steve McQueen was so shriveled with cancer he looked pregnant." She wanted to sip a mug of steaming coffee and savor the morning's normal dreariness: typewriters clacking, the low hum of voices through paper-thin partitions. "What do you do, read old newspapers?" she asked. "What does any of that stuff have to do with you?" She stared from her tiny window overlooking the Loop, gnawing on Bruce's remarks for signs of malice or spite. "Look, Lydia, come see me for Christmas. I want you here. New York is Andy Warhol, Chicago is Norman Rockwell. Come eat some Campbell's Soup." Shoppers in the street, dressed in rusk and autumn greens, held down skirts and finger-brushed hair in a losing battle with a brisk wind. "I love you, Lyd. Come east, come swim like a dolphin."

✳

Lydia rocked, alone on the porch swing, a pack of cigarettes and a lighter by her side, trying to inhabit the present like a richly-papered room with a view. Wind ebbed and flowed. Her mother's old two-story house, nestled in a neighborhood protected by the largest private police force in the country, the University of Chicago cadets, creaked in counterpoint to rusty squeaking chains. She tried to let her thoughts seep into shady spaces between her nerves. Even on the commuter train from Hyde Park to the Loop each morning, her fear of strangers made her absent-minded. What was I thinking? she would wonder, distracted by the smooth electric click of the train, its familiar odor of vinyl and rubber, afterscent of perfume and perspiration. The stations passed with a squeal of brakes, an afterimage of wooden platforms, mile posts clicking past like metronomes.

*

"Lydia," Robin said in the kitchen. She was munching on a piece of French bread. "All day I've dealt with nerds, stupids, idiots, morons, imbeciles, dwarfs, and dufuses." She caught her breath. "Even a turd or two. Let's go somewhere, we can leave a trail of breadcrumbs for the birds to eat all up." Lydia sipped her coffee. "You've earned a mouthful of soap with that language." Robin leafed through the magazine on the kitchen table. "How to survive with a man. How to survive without a man. What to do with cellulite. How to know when he's unfaithful. Danger signs of drugs." She made a face. "Lydia, either you read that junk all evening or spend quality time with your kid. It's a three-minute world, my teacher always says. Is that all the time you're going to give me?" They decided on ice cream. Lydia's mother was dozing in the love seat, her whitened hair sprayed with silver shifting light from an old movie. Standing near her, Lydia became giddy and leaned against the door frame. "Let's go," Robin said, grabbing her hand. Lydia felt like a refugee, arriving in time for the new era of television, of machines propelled through air by nothing but high-octane fuel, of computers full of private investigations. "It's Humphrey Bogart," she said. "Shouldn't we stay and watch?"

When they returned, her mother had switched on the ceiling lights, something she rarely did, and stood next to her chair, facing the door, her arms folded across her chest. Through the window, streetlight splashed and glimmered among unraked leaves. Humphrey Bogart, trench-coated, walked across the tarmac in the rain. "It's Bruce," Claire said. "You'd better call." "Did Bogart kill somebody, Claire?" Robin asked. "What is it?" Lydia said, adrenaline pumping. "He's in the hospital. The number's next to the phone."

Someone had peppered him with rice and buckshot from a sawed-off shotgun. The aim had been awry, though, and most of the grains of rice didn't even penetrate the skin. But his eyes were bandaged, and there could be some permanent damage. "I know it's late, Lydia," Bruce said, "but I want you here. There's something weird with my karma. I need you."

✳

Lydia rocked on the porch in early light until Natasha arrived to take her to the airport. "A sawed-off shotgun, Lydia? I thought those creeps used Saturday-night specials." She squeezed Lydia's hand. "He sounds fine. A little trauma might do him some good, if you know what I mean. Cool him down, maybe. If you don't watch color TV, you start to think the grass is black." Lydia drummed her fingers on the leather seatcover of the BMW. She stared at the blue-white sparks of a rocking commuter train beside the highway. "You're talking gibberish. Anyway, it's the flying. All I can think about is that."

"Well, don't worry. Thousands of planes fly every day. O'Hare's the busiest in the world." An emergency van streaked past, lights flashing, horn bleeping. "Oh, great," Lydia said. "Planes fly every day, right? So there's no risk?" She put a cigarette back in its box and chewed her fingernail.

Natasha started talking about EST—Erhard Seminar Training. "Werner asks a really profound question. Suppose you were sent from the planet Mars to Earth to help everyone live better, and suppose you couldn't go home until you succeeded. What would you do?"

At the airport, she stepped into a dream that didn't end until she returned to Chicago. She tried to listen to her heartbeat above the roar of the engine. A baby cried behind her. Each pop song on the earphones took her three minutes closer to a safe landing. Frank Sinatra, Jack Jones, Don Ho. Each cigarette was part of a chain she could hold between her fingers. Coffin nails, holding the plane together as it tunneled into the light of morning. Up, down. Three minutes. She tried chanting, a trick Bruce practiced. I love my life, I love my life, I love my life. I love Robin, I love my mother. I love Bruce.

A three-minute country. The stewardess offered her coffee and juice, a chocolate doughnut. She refused with a tight plum of a smile.

Reaching over might upset the equilibrium on some invisible level. Everything was going so well. At cruising altitude, there were brief calm moments, but a passage through turbulence forced all passengers to return to their seats and fasten their belts. "I've never had it this bad," someone said. "Oh yeah?" a second passenger answered. "Once, the engine fell off on my way to Phoenix. They're designed to do that, you know." Lydia's blood rushed from her veins to soft tissue where it didn't belong. The plane was streaking above the clouds like a javelin or rocket that had only so much thrust before it descended, engines kaput. Cling to the music, she thought. Maintain composure. Besides, the other passengers, reading *Forbes* and *Fortune,* looked like advertisements for safe travel.

Everything moved in slow-motion, and backwards. The boy she left at the fraternity ball returned to ask her to dinner. She accepted. In the restaurant his face turned shiny like polished metal. "Your place or mine, babe? You owe me one," he slurred. "More than three days without a piece, I go crazy." She stalked away, still in slow-motion. On the plane, her face reddened with original anger. "How dare you!" she wanted to scream. Instead she returned to the tape. "Wear my lei to the luau, sweetheart/ While I strum out sweet love in your ears."

3.

At last the plane found its landing pattern, thumped to the ground, and braked with a huge rush of wind. At the gate, Bruce's friend Tom was waiting in a red windbreaker. "The Upper East and the Village are full of neurotics," he said as they drove. "In the West it's hip and holy." Lydia locked her smile into place and watched their progress into the city, along the flank of the Hudson River. *The one you smack is the one you keep.* Memories, bits of music, phrases, the dancing dementos. Decompression, she thought, smoothing her skirt, clutching the shoulder-strap of her purse, her heart pacing the floor of her chest.

"You know, Lyd," Bruce told her the night before he left, "you never really understand anything you say, do you?" She had stared at him, her eyes beginning to water with anger and hurt. "What do you mean? I'm blurting out my heart and you tell me I don't mean what I say?" He dismissed her anger with a wave of his hand. "No, you're not speaking from the heart." It was his last item in a withering litany of accusations. "You *never* speak from the heart. You always speak from the nerves." His remark gave her pause. "The heart isn't a nerve?" "It's a *muscle*. What happened, Lyd, you sleep through Biology 101?"

The heart a muscle! Imagine that. A muscle, beating in my chest.

Bruce was asleep in the hospital bed, so helpless with his eyes bandaged that he made her dizzy. She stroked the dark hairs on his head and bent for a kiss, reaching past the hospital's antiseptic buzz. His distinctive spiciness tickled her nose like ginger beneath the odor of antiseptic and hospital sheets.

His fingers pressed into the small of her back. "I'm not really asleep!" he said. "In fact, I wrote a poem just now, in my head. 'The blackbird/ has blue/ bruises.' What you think?" Her fingers trailed down his arm, then touched the tape, the patches of gauze on his eyes. "Does it hurt?"

"It's like looking into nothing," he said, fingers drumming the bedsheet. "I feel like I'm in a cage. Nothing is all I see." He motioned for his glass of water. Lydia reached past the gifts on the bedside table: a nosegay, a pretty pastel card, bright Matisse cutouts, a bottle of soap bubbles. "My karma owed me something. It was out there, waiting. You read the news, watch the tube, sniff the air." Lydia's nerves were filling with frantic energy. "Robin says everyone has a three-minute attention span," she said. "Cigarettes, songs, newspapers, attention spans. We're in and out of everything." "A shotgun blast," he shrugged. "That's not even three *seconds*." He looked towards her as though he could see. "But better than a sucking chest wound in a firefight, huh? How's Robin, by the way?"

"She's . . . "

"The punk appeared out of nowhere. Fucking Dodge City. I screamed my banshee scream and went for the mace." "That's terrible," Lydia said. "No, just *different,* Lyd. A test. You know, a *test?* The doors of perception are always open, we've just got to be receptive. *Receptive,* Lyd. Our minds aren't located, the culture just makes us think so. We have to find etheric webs, power points, the seeds of an emerging world. After all, we *create* whatever's around us."

Her palms were sweating. "What about your graffiti, your murals? I thought that's why you were here."

"New York is fast, frantic, full of ancient wisdom. *Ancient* wisdom, Lyd, older than the sun. The Midwest can stifle our chakras. But here, I'm ageless and I'm also new. The dawn of a new age, great spiritual masters, a world teacher emerging. Can you *understand* that? I mean, we call him The Christ, here in the West, but he's all of us, and he's emerging, manifesting."

She caressed the plaid folds of her skirt. "What if you had died?"

"Lyd, don't take it so *personal*. Can't you see what I'm saying?"

"I'm *trying*. Can't you see I'm trying? What about your book? What about your family?"

Bruce slapped himself, as though waking up to the world's absurdity. "Hey, babe, we don't need sarcasm. That's negative nihilism, which destroys cosmic energy, which is not only bad for the soul, but for the planet. Anyway, it's the *psychic bond* that counts. I can't understand graffiti unless I breathe the place that makes it happen. New York *is* graffiti."

"Can't things just stop?"

"That's death, Lyd. Don't feel bad. Put a rock in your shoe."

"What?"

"Put a *rock* in your shoe." He leaned forward, preaching with conviction. "When you've got a *rock* to worry about, that's all you know. You forget the rest."

"That's a wonderful idea. Why don't I slash my wrists? Why don't I put leeches on my back? Why don't I stick a toothpick in my ear?"

"A toothpick wouldn't help," Bruce said. "You're getting sarcastic again." Bruce would come to her, unwilled, in other guises, but she knew she would always imagine him with a plank of sunlight laid across the hospital sheets, his head alert as though studying the room through white circles of gauze. He folded his hands together and brought the tips of his fingers to his mouth. "No arguing. Hey. Let's not argue. Let's just meditate. No separations, Lyd. No duality. Okay?"

She stayed in his small room uptown, memories stretched around her like a net—keepsakes, scraps of manuscript, snapshots of murals.

One, labeled "the goddess *Wisdom*," was almost classical, nothing like the geometric social realism of the WPA Depression murals in Chicago. A veiled Beaux-Arts woman with fat fingers held a pale pinkish globe of the world in her hands. Her eyes were heavy and she seemed to be in a trance.

✳

"Funny thing," said Natasha. "I was waiting, you know, I was *watching myself waiting*. Even here, trying to escape the comfort cycle. It was like, I was fighting to get free of nature and history, make myself over, know what I mean? Should I have a smoke? Yes, no. No, yes." Lydia, pasty-faced, bloated, pointed to an escalator in the airport lobby. "Let's get my bag," she said. The plane had been as hot and stuffy as an oven, the turbulence intolerable.

On the highway, Natasha sat on her horn to force a slow-moving truck into another lane. "Well," Natasha said. "Long-term commitments are worth the trouble, but not the boredom. That's it, in a nutshell. Don't you realize how much boredom a long commitment absorbs? I saw a statistic somewhere, and it was gruesome. The arguments aren't bad, they give a rush, clean out your system. It's the dead spots that kill." She squeezed Lydia's knee. "Hey, if it don't work, fix it. If it can't be fixed, throw it away. Life is too short for grief. Lawyer, shrink, voodoo man, whatever works." She angled onto the exit ramp. "Go with the flow."

Whatever works. Go with the flow. Lydia shrugged.

"Let's have lunch, Lydia. Let's have lunch at a New Age restaurant I've heard about." Lydia thought: go with the flow. "New Age, huh?" Natasha sounded full of something new, something a little wild. "You know, new age, new experiences. New Age music, New Age crystals, New Age food. All that good stuff. It's good to try everything these days, even in Chicago where so many people are pigs. So many experiences out there."

"Why?" Lydia asked, truly curious at last. "Why is it good to try everything?" There's not really any way home anymore, she thought, but that's where I'm going. Not the same place, though. She wanted a good cry.

85

"That's an odd question," Natasha finally said. "I mean, I didn't expect to have to explain. But I guess it's just nice to rest your *being* in new experiences. You know, let yourself be taken, um, wherever."

✳

"Lydia," Robin said, "how do we forget things?"

Lydia ran her finger along the rough grain of the porch swing. "You mean like raking leaves?"

"Pay attention, Lydia. How do we *forget* things?" Robin spit on her watercolor brush and rubbed it dry on a sheet of old newspaper.

"All right. Actually, we don't forget anything. It's just that lots of things get buried and we can't remember them."

"Oh." She locked the brush in her tin of paints and closed her sketch pad. "Well, I'm going inside to see what Claire figured out to do. She said she'd take me on an adventure today."

"Why did you ask?"

She crushed the newspaper into a ball. "I knew you'd want to know, Lydia." She squeezed the ball of paper and tossed it to her mother. "Anyway, now that I've figured out how to paint the things I miss, I was wondering how to paint the things I forget."

"So what did you do? Leave the page blank? Cover it with thick lines?" Robin giggled and wandered inside. There it is, the whole kit and caboodle, Lydia thought. She pushed herself backwards far enough to get the swing going. Upstairs she heard a medley of Beatles songs on Robin's cassette player. One of the Beatles belted out "Yellow Submarine" in a beer-hall baritone. Lydia was tempted to let herself drift into the past, to those days when she and Bruce sang along to such ditties. Instead, she reeled forward, then back, then forward again, and for a moment stopped thinking, swung without a care in the world. Then she wondered, staring at the trunk of a large oak, how it might feel to live the rest of her life in a forest.

WORLD POETRY SLAM

J ane Jefferson entered The Black Factory, the bar hosting the Slam, in a white cotton turtleneck, white pants, and a pair of white jogging shoes. The drinkers gave her a round of applause.— Listening to you, baby, is better than good sex, someone yelled. Hear, hear, Peter Draper thought, wondering how he might judge the match without letting his emotions come into play. Jefferson could move in a snap from an anti-establishment jazz rap into a slowdance love croon that whispered in the eaves.

Then Kafka walked in and the temperature rose a few degrees. Kafka is a big man who's lifted his share of weights and lived through a bevy of cold alley fights, who's cracked a few heads (mostly before he climbed onto the AA twelve-step wagon, before he found that tattered crucial paperback of beat poetry), who's had his own noggin raked across the sidewalk a few times. Dressed in black T-shirt, black corduroys, and old black sneakers, he made his way to the bar. A pre-fight hush descended on the room. Only the clink of a glass or a muffled conversation survived the babble of a moment before. Wherever he stood, leaning against the bar with a ginger ale or huddling forward, good ear tilted to the speaking voice, he looked ready to stagger his listener with a one-two punch, first a portrait of an alkie, evicted from his room so the owner could rehab, then an elegy to a friend lost in the high mountain sierras or Cleveland, he wasn't sure which.

They both wanted Draper as a judge. He didn't know why, maybe because he had that look, like a young Kerouac after a binge. That night, he wore a green eyeshade. He had worked once in a telegraph office, he knew the cost of words. Working with words, working with money, what difference? Waste was easy, either way. Attention must be paid, to the lilt of syllables, the clink of coins, the clock different from the one that told the time of day.

A knockout was possible but unlikely. It happened often enough in the Slam's early days, but Kafka and Jefferson were pros, the reformed drunk with the will of a successful politician, the challenger with the voice of a songbird who knew the streets like the tattoo of a robin's egg on her wrist, who chanted an audience into a happiness so complete they floated from their chairs. Love medicine. Draper himself went against her once, when the Slam was new—no cameras, no lights, no coverage on the 10 o'clock news, only a smoky near-empty bar with old *Life* magazines decoupaged and lacquered to the walls. Waltzing around the stage, Jane put him away in the first, rapping out rage at "whiskey sister heaven/ slowdancing in the nude," then seducing the drunks with a rhapsody about "sweetbaby bobby." Draper tried to slink away after the knockout, but she and Kafka sat him down for a beer and taught him the ropes. He had to forget everything before he could stay in the ring for long with a slammer.

The three judges sat in folding chairs at a sawhorse table near the stage. Besides Draper, there was a thick-chested industrial technician with a zigzag scar on his right cheek, and a stubby German woman in training to be a French chef. With felt-tip pens and notepads, they could give a poet anywhere from one to ten. Ten rounds, a winner each round, with 150 people in a space for 50. MTV was there, a kleig light turned The Black Factory into a funhouse of shadows. The director pushed aside chipped wooden tables to make room for Kafka, known for backstepping across the small plyboard stage into the crowd of drunks, drifters, and night poets. They worked the loading docks, assembled steel filing cabinets by day, wrote poems in their heads to the rhyme and meter of the assembly lines. Tuesday nights, they came to the Slam, jabbed, feinted, went for the knockout with stanzas scrawled on invoices, chants written on bar napkins.

Kafka took the stage first to a silent chorus of raised fists.— Everything is rhythm, he told Draper after the young poet's first-round knockout, and now he proved it. "Stay away from the goddamn/ neighborhood/ You punk!/ Listen to the gurgle of a carburetor,/ a tailpipe tongued into your ear!" The sweat sluiced from his receding hairline into creases above his eyebrows. He stalked the stage, hands gripping a baseball bat in pantomime. Draper felt like he was pumping a stationary bicycle just to keep up, even though it was over quick, Draper snapping awake as though from a nap on the afternoon bus, the hoots and whistles making clear who had the first round.

Jane took a final toke from the hand-rolled business she was smoking. "I/ am/ Jane Jefferson." Her words pulsated with erotic monkey-shines. "I am Jane Jefferson/ and this is/ the poem/ you don't read/ aloud/ is the one/ about your dog/ and his exquisite bone/ a bone/ that melts/ in the steam bath/ the soft pelting of steam/ the hair around the bone/ it's/ guaranteed." Draper had to doodle with his pen to recover from the way she stoked each syllable, but finally the big man's dementia carried things, especially with the help of the young chef, who gave him an eight and a half.

Draper had the feeling that Jane was only sparring, though, feeling out her man, getting his number. Sure enough, she hugged Kafka and scatted to the stage. Draper couldn't make sense of her words, a chant foreign to his ears, he only listened, enraptured, to her seductive fingertip voice. She stopped in the middle of a phrase. The silence was all the more audible. He had trouble coming back to the world. Even the young chef rubbed her eyes. Kafka strode across the spongy plyboard and tried to punch away the trance. "On the corner of/ Colfax and Montaigne/ I see a zero in a coat and tie/ He's singing the 'Hallelujah Chorus'! " Still some zap, still rope-a-dope, still the zingers, but Jane won hands down.

The match went that way, strength against strength. Draper forgot who he was. Time became a series of tides: low tide, high tide, breakwater, beach. No mathematics, no numbers, only poems, not even words, and in the tenth Kafka was down 5-4. He needed the tie to keep his title, he pulled out all the stops, lip curled, voice like gravel. Images of a boxer collided like boxcars with a maimed soldier, a penny-ante huckster on the last roll of his dice, and everywhere the boxer, battered, bruised, still on his feet. "America, you have fed me pinecones and leather for breakfast/ You have taught me the alphabet and gotten it wrong/ You have climbed to the top of the Tower/ wrapped in a flag/ and pushed me/ and I dived/ into the Loop/ the endless Loop/ the endless Loop." He got a standing ovation. His performance was instant legend for the regulars, something to take them back to the sixties, but Draper was young and gave Kafka a nine.

Jane took her time, she *emigrated,* sauntering with slow honey in her slim hips (eyes half-closed), found her spot, stood still, absolutely still for the first time. Draper held his breath, the industrial technician went "whoa, baby," and the young chef, the third judge, folded her arms, caressed her own shoulders. "My lover's/ making me over/ again," Jane whispered, snapping her fingers, then launching into a chant to obscenity, "a rap and rag/ of every kind of obscenity/ known to woman or man,/ every kind of obscenity/ on the face of the earth:/ the obscenity of *in*equality,/ the obscenity of *apart*heid,/ the obscenity of bad sex,/ the obscenity of *soft* drinks,/ the obscenity of p.o.w. poverty,/ the obscenity of wealth,/ the obscenity of good sex/ as sweet as sour pork,/ the obscenity of *angels,/* the obscenity of/ birds,/ the obscenity of no sex at all/ as sour as the *colored* ink/ of the Sunday comics/ or the lingerie ads, /the sweet obscenity of Satan,/ the obscenity of a *ball*-/ point pen that doesn't work,/ the obscenity of a poem/ that does." She finished the rap, slow love song to the world, and Draper gave the first ten in the history of the Slam. The technician gave her a nine, and even the chef shaved only half a point from that.

The crowd dispersed quickly, maybe because the joint was too crowded for sociable drinking. Kafka hated to lose and headed for the door, but Draper cut him off, sat him down for a ginger ale.— Some match. On points I thought you won, but something happened there at the end.

—You got transported, Kafka said, drumming his fingers on the scarred table, studying the place with short quick swings of his head. — You forgot where you were, what you were doing. All your theory disappeared.

— How'd you know?

— Same thing happened to me. Think I'm *immune?*

— Words don't add up.

— So, congratulations. You might be a poet yet.

They talked, listening to subliminal texture, the way words traveled. Kafka ignored the MTV director, who wanted an interview, ignored the slummers in their soft silks who wanted to know him before he became a movie star or a singer with a rock group. Kafka and Draper kept talking to each other, after a while Jane came over. All three did two things at once, they talked, really talked, they paid attention, but they also made up poems in their heads, Jane a poem to Walter Payton, Kafka a poem to Ezzard Charles, Draper a poem in prose to the poetry slam.

RACCOONS

With Deb asleep in her mother's room, Hugh climbed the stairs and listened past the ringing in his ears. Empty beds settled into floorboards. Other suspicious sounds scratched away at the night's peace. It took Hugh a minute to understand what he was hearing—a whole family of raccoons in the crawlspace that tunneled alongside the hallway. They cried out in pleasure, ticking claws over cardboard boxes filled with decades of family artifacts. Unmarried, Hugh and Deb had given up a small expensive apartment in Chicago and moved to her mother's house in the suburbs. Her mother lived in the Bahamas as a companion to a wealthier woman; divorced, she could afford to keep her house only if she didn't live in it. But she was too attached to it to put it on the market. It was 1980, that kind of year for all three of them, and for lots of other people, too.

Downstairs, Hugh found Deb's schoolgirl encyclopedia on an un-dusted mahogany shelf. Raccoons, he read, are so determined in their bandit way to endure that in man's absence the earth might well become their domain. The message frightened him a little. Their garbage-can raids came like clockwork every night, and neither Deb nor Hugh was much good at fending them off. The two of them had enough trouble just getting to work each day, arriving at the station seconds before the train pulled from the platform, where they joined thousands of other commuters.

"The Humane Society can put traps around the yard," Hugh said the next day, leaning on the horn. They were caught on the expressway in rush-hour traffic after missing the train. "We should have waited for the next goddamn train." He tapped the horn.

"That won't do any good."

"It won't get us to the Loop any faster, but it might help my blood pressure." He reached for a cigarette.

"By the way," she said quietly, "I'm still waiting for my period. I was a little nauseated this morning."

"They were at the window." Hugh massaged his chest, poking between the right ribs because something was sore. He tried to remember cancer's seven warning signs.

"What?"

"The raccoons, Deb. What are we talking about?"

"Look, get in the right lane," she said, drumming the briefcase on her lap. "You mind dropping me off? I'm late."

"No, I don't mind. I can be the one who spends an hour looking for a parking space, even though it's your turn."

"Just park underground. I'll pay."

A few days later, Deb's pregnancy a fact of life, Hugh threw away his pack of cigarettes on the wooden platform of the suburban station. Everyone waiting was cloaked in the dull colors of freeze-dry vegetables.

"Good for you," Deb said, rolling her eyes. She opened her mouth in a toothy parody of a scream.

The passengers, lost in their *Wall Street Journals* or *Tribunes*, were scoping out the day's headlines. Hugh didn't even bother to read over their shoulders. Now, he lives in a small town and misses the glamour of big-city dailies, but that December he always slung a mystery into his briefcase. He didn't want to get any closer to reality than Robert Parker's Spenser or Raymond Chandler's Philip Marlowe could take him.

They glided past grain-storage elevators and high-power lines. The sky was the color of granite. "About the raccoons," he said. "What are we going to do?"

"Raccoons?" She squinted. With her pregnancy and his hypochondria, they lived half in the world and half in their fears, and their non sequiturs were standard-issue.

"The cubs were at the window watching me read, on their hind legs, noses against the glass, tiny black buttons on their snouts."

"To hell with raccoons," she said. They were passing through the city's industrial belt. "What are we going to do about this baby?" Beyond an endless file of Inland Steel freight cars and tree-lined tracks, long aisles of World War II vintage cottages and bungalows went to seed along with idle factories: quonset huts of galvanized steel, some as long as football fields, and dark brick buildings with unpainted facades, rust-red smokestacks, and cracked windows.

At its downtown dock, the train braked to a noisy electric crawl. Deb looked sick; everyone else, already angling for exits, ruffled paper, snapped shut briefcases, and wiggled into coats. They pushed forward into the echoing chilliness of a concrete areaway. On the stairs, Deb clutched the metal rail so fiercely her fingers turned milky.

Inside the terminal, spongy with echoes, Hugh could taste fried eggs, dusty linoleum, and grease. Deb repeated her question. "It's totally up to you," he answered. "You want the baby, fine. You don't want it, fine." Anyone can talk about anything in a city crowd with little fear of discovery, but he lowered his voice, raised his chin, and glanced to either side. He tucked his briefcase under one arm and flexed his fingers, as though ready for a martial arts demonstration in the dingy corridor between Feski's Donut Shop and the flower kiosk. "It's up to you. You're carrying it. You're the one who won't have so many options. How does that saying go? 'A buggy in the hall is the enemy of freedom'?"

"That's real fair," she said. "You ever hear of shared responsibility? It's a brand-new concept."

They pushed through a smudged glass door. "What's not fair is for a man to tell a woman what to do in a situation like this." At the end of a long concrete tunnel full of candy wrappers and cigarette butts, escalators climbed to the street. A bearded man with a long stocking cap and cracked leather jacket blew on his saxophone, his head tilted into "Imagine," the John Lennon song. It was a radio standard, but not the sort of thing that sounded great on sax, especially

94

with concrete echoing its refrain. Deb stepped to one side and searched her big coat pocket among ticket stubs, bus transfers, breath mints, and notes scribbled to herself until she found two quarters. She tossed them into the saxophonist's instrument case. There was real money in it, lots of bills and a jumble of coins. People weren't usually so generous, especially to a lone sax player, offkey even to Hugh's un-tutored ears.

His music faded in the bustle of street-level noise. After a soggy glance and a perfunctory peck on the cheek, Deb crossed Randolph Street with the light. Hugh turned casually to the newspaper kiosk, nestled beneath the imposing Italian Renaissance design of the Chicago Public Library and Cultural Center, and saw the headline: JOHN LENNON SLAIN.

He bought the tabloid. Surrounded by the usual crowd of freaks, small-time hustlers, and derelicts waiting for the library to open, he read about the murder, absorbing every gruesome detail. Other bystanders, like himself, were neatly attired, obviously on the way to an office in a tall building, but their eyes told the real story. They didn't live where they worked, or even where they lived, but in some staging area of the mind, making raids on the way things had turned out.

"Let's have a moment of silence for poor John Lennon," Hugh said at the office, holding up the paper. Everyone looked askance, a little embarrassed. "To tell you the truth," one senior copywriter said, "I didn't even know that guy was still around." "Yeah," Hugh mumbled, "he was still around." Though they mostly gathered dust, Hugh owned every album Lennon made after the Beatles broke up, so he had lunch with Tom Hogan, a closet socialist with thinning hair. They stood at Berghoff's polished mahogany counter, munch-ing on sausages and drinking beer. "You know, I subscribe to *Playboy*—mostly for the interviews," Tom said between bites of sausage. "So I knew Lennon was back. I read the interview there."

They speculated on his years of silence. "He was a househusband," Tom said. "He brought up his son." Hugh told him about *Sgt. Pep-per's Lonely Hearts Club Band*. "I'd put the speakers loud and lie there on my parents' bedspread, one of those tufted chenille things. I was waiting for enlightenment." He grunted when Tom grinned. "I ended up losing a little hearing. My left ear rings all the time now."

Tom adjusted his glasses. "I didn't pay that much attention. Folk music was my thing. I'd sit in Earl's in New Town or drive to New York and camp in the Village. Everybody screamed over the Beatles, I listened to Dylan, Ray and Glover, Paxton, Phil Ochs." He took a sip of beer and wiped a smidgin of mustard from his lip. "Then Lennon got political. I paid attention to *that*." He adjusted his glasses again. "I've got to say, though, even if the timing's wrong, that he was never a socialist. Not really."

That afternoon Deb was exhausted, her hair lank. Until they reached their stop, Hugh buried himself in the papers, hypnotized by the murder, reciting details. She waved him off, a little breathless. "Who wants to hear it? Here one minute, gone the next. Some guy decides to do you in, and that's it." She was still shaking her head when they queued up to leave the train. "Whatever happens doesn't matter, until something happens you can't change. Then you spend your life regretting."

"Are we still talking about Lennon?"

"Who knows?" she said, biting a nail.

They had the abortion. They walked into a low-slung building with bars on the windows and she did it. Afterwards, Hugh lay on Deb's mother's mattress, his hands behind his head, and thought of things to say, but he never said them. Deb's regret was for the family they decided against; he regretted the need to decide in the first place. But she was so distraught he finally promised her they would get pregnant again soon.

He also became obsessed with the raccoons. He was a zealot. They had to go. Someone told him they hated loud music, so he positioned big speakers at either end of the crawl space and blasted guitar riffs into it: the Stones, the Dead, Led Zeppelin, Ten Years After, Jimi Hendrix, even the Beatles and Bob Dylan. When that didn't work, he called the outfit the Humane Society recommended. They filled the yard with cages. The cages trapped a possum, a rabbit, and one large male raccoon.

Hugh followed the Lennon story in the dailies, the news weeklies, the rock magazines, and even supermarket tabloids. One printed a photo of his pale face in the morgue, hair combed back, features at rest. The thing played itself out, finally fading even from the back pages, but sometimes Hugh dreamed about him, and, one day while it snowed, he played Lennon's last album, *Double Fantasy,* and stared from the window.

Then they caught one of the babies. All night it yelped plaintively in the cage near their bedroom window, and at dawn Hugh went out with a long stick. The mother, coiled above him on the largest limb of an oak, hissed. Deb, still in her post-abortion funk, stared from the window. With the stick Hugh poked the cage door until it sprung open. The baby darted into a tunnel under the bedroom. The mother, still ferocious, backed in after it. The whole family set up housekeeping there.

In Hugh's dreams, Lennon's murder became a mistake. He had a new album out and went on tour loose-limbed in a T-shirt and jeans, baking bread between sets, his wife and child on stage with him. He sang a new song, a rousing anthem of freedom whose dream lyrics echoed through the concert hall. But something happened to Lennon in the middle of the last chorus. His voice lost its vigor and settled like silt into river deeps. Maybe it was the bright lights, maybe the way Hugh's eyes blinked and blurred, but Lennon's features dissolved into silly putty, melting in bright indoor heat, and when Hugh could see again, he recognized *himself* on stage, and woke a little sick, a little angry. He tried to remember the lyrics to the dream anthem, thinking maybe he could find a way to record it, but the words were trapped on the tip of his tongue like the name of somebody he knew a long time ago, maybe even cared about, but couldn't remember to save his life.

SIDEWALKS WHITE LIKE BONES

Annie was a ballerina. She spent a lot of time alone.

"How come you're here?" she wanted to know when Doug arrived in Louisiana, exhausted after two days of driving. "I thought we agreed not to see one another." Her voice low, resigned, she removed her garden gloves and tapped a spade until it was free of moist soil.

"So we did." She had moved to Denver with him, then returned south with her husband Randy. "My actions have little to do with our relationship," she had said. *"That* will continue, whatever the distance between us. But there's work to do."

"Does that work have anything to do with Randy?"

"Look, Doug, I can't respond to that kind of low energy. Trust me."

Now she paused on the balls of her feet, as though ready to stretch before rehearsal room mirrors, and settled into a lotus position. "Why are you here? At this particular time?"

"I love you."

"What kind of reason is that, Doug?"

He stared at her. "I just thought it would be nice."

" 'Be nice.' Is that how you decide what to do?"

"Why not?"

"We're not our likes and dislikes. I don't mean to sound harsh, but you're a grownup. You know better than that."

"I've come a long way to see you."

"Of course I'm glad of that. You're my spiritual brother." She stared at the grass between them. "But I think you're still trapped in low energy."

"Annie, I've really been traveling a long time."

She smiled. "We've all been traveling, for centuries."

How could he argue? He wanted to be with her because he loved her, but she didn't want to hear that. He felt like—oops, here I go, recording what I feel, identifying with my emotions.

✳

My room has a large bay window. Outside the sky is the color of clouds. Cold weather has arrived. It's drizzling. In the schoolyard across the street children play on covered walks—got-you-last, red-light, ring-around-the-rosie.

Tangle, my goldfinch, rushes from her cage with a whisper of black wings and perches on a book called *Truth*. The Jehovah's Witnesses, a whole family of blacks in Sunday attire, brought it to my door. My neighbor across the hall had threatened to sic his dobermans on them, so maybe they expected another rebuff. The group's patriarch, an old man with white hair and skin creased like shoe leather, scratched his head and studied my face. He could tell I was wide-eyed, at sea in the world, and he asked, "What is eternal life? How can we live in peace and happiness? Why is the world filled with trouble?"

Embarrassed at being found out, I grabbed the blue book held open before me and slammed the door. After some whispering, the patriarch cleared his throat. "Sir, we'd like a donation."

Playful now, I slipped a dime under the door. He cleared his throat again, as though to curse my threshold with a wad of spit, then they went away. The echoes of the man's dark wing-tip shoes and his wife's high heels faded, leaving nothing but indecipherable silence.

When I skimmed through the book, there were footnotes in it from *Look* magazine. Now floorboards creak and water gurgles in the pipes—the girl next door is preparing for work. She looks so much like Annie—does she spend her evenings with esoteric books, weighing the wisdom she finds?

It's late. I should get to work.

No. I'll start again.

✳

This is a story about Annie. She sent Doug a letter yesterday: "I am not my emotions, Doug. I am not my relationships with others. I am not my ideas. I am not my experiences. I am something else. What, I'm not sure about. But I don't *have* to be friendly. I don't even have to smile. I'm not trying to exclude you, but to include others. Do you think I'm crazy? If not, please send me some good energy. I *need* it." In the letter was an owl feather; Doug placed it on the dashboard of his car. There was a P.S.: "My number one priority is racing consciousness. (Can you believe that? I was going to scratch it out and write the word I meant to write, which was *raising,* of course—but I thought it too funny to scratch out. Freudian slip.)"

Sometimes she lives alone, in a one-room cottage near the Bayou Teche, sometimes in town with her husband Randy. Once, the three of them—Annie, Randy, Doug—lived together, renting a big tilted place with three bedrooms which has since been demolished to make way for a row of townhouses. Randy slept alone there, unaware that Annie and Doug were lovers. In the morning Odessa, her golden retriever, would nudge them awake before he discovered them together.

Let me start again.

✳

I shut the window and turn on the radio. After a minute it brings me the world's tinny message: a love song! Paul and Linda McCartney singing "It's Just Another Day." I laugh and sing along. I slap my knee.

The schoolbell rings. Some of the children, protected by earmuffs and winter gear, continue to play in the cold. The rain's stopped, but the sky is grayer. I pour a glass of orange juice and listen to the radiator. I'm not going to work. The Jehovah's Witnesses might be in the bushes, birch rods in hands, wing-tip shoes giving them away. No, I don't believe that, and I'm tired of my playfulness. I'm not going because I want to think about Annie. I miss her so much. I spend most of my time waiting for her—I live a small life, study sidewalk cracks, and stare into the street.

A man who looks a lot like my grandfather is standing at the edge of the schoolyard in a windbreaker. He fingers his few strands of white hair and then grips the chain-link fence.

Tangle, back in her cage, cracks seeds and chirps. When her mate Mossy disappeared through an open window, Annie and I spent hours discussing whether to free Tangle, too. A few of Annie's friends, in headbands and drawstring pants, were outraged at the very *idea* of a caged bird. They celebrated Mossy's flight. But we decided Tangle would never survive in the natural world.

There's danger in this room, in its ticking silence. It is here, the silence says, it is here. Annie would say a memory from a past life, or a voice from the invisible world, tried to reach me, but that my soul wasn't subtle enough. "You are it, Doug, you are it." Could that be true? I don't know how to think about the spiritual life. When she slept beside me, she would tunnel into her pillow toward the source of all wisdom, the moon bathing her dark shoulders and thick tangled hair. A Buddhist altar stood witness near the birdcage. On our waterbed, every slight turn jostled us together. Like Mossy and Tangle, I thought, we would follow our happiness together; the complicated canvas of the world would change into primary colors and whirl us away.

✳

She was always able to recall each of her dreams in detail. I can't remember mine, Doug would complain. "But you're not your dreams, Doug." Playfully scolding, still in another world, she would smile. "You know better than that."

Annie, Doug thought, I know I'm not only my dreams, and certainly not only my ideas. And yes, I can accept I'm not only my emotions. Hallelujah! But not my relationships to others?

"No, Doug," she said once as they sat in the park, feeding ducks in a small pond. "I think you misunderstand the nature of invisible things."

"Look," he said, squinting into the shadows. "There's some kind of invisible *thing* eating the bread."

She stared. "Can you see what it is?"

"No. The water's too muddy." They threw more bread. "Look! Whatever it is got one of the *ducks*."

She folded her cotton dirndl around her legs. "You poking fun?"

A delivery truck downshifted nearby. The conversation died and they looked for pebbles, the ones bright like coins. They scrubbed their hands against the bark of butternut trees and waited on the curb for traffic to clear. She leaned forward, hands on her dancer's thighs.

Annie, how *do* we define ourselves? Isn't contact necessary?

Let me start again.

✳

"Would you like to come back to Denver and dance?"

"Well, I don't know if I should tell you this," Annie said, "but I had a dream. I was dancing in a large studio. There was snow outside."

"You'd be welcome. More than welcome. We'd both have privacy. You'd dance, I'd work. In any case, I made a decision. I've decided I won't return here, not for a while, but I'll leave a space in my life for you."

"Thank you, Doug." She painted a Christmas card. He leafed through record albums and put something by Joni Mitchell on the stereo. Outside, bare branches grazed against the shingles of her cottage. "Did you bring the weather with you from Denver?"

She was surrounding a charcoal-colored angel with an aura. The half-finished card rested on a miniature easel. "Roy G. Biv," he said.

"Who?"

"No, what. The colors of the rainbow." He started scribbling. "Doug."

"Shush. I'm writing something for you."

"Doug, I tell you what: why don't you write something for me?"

"With love and squalor?"

She frowned. "You call this squalor?"

"I was joking."

"Naturally." She unbraided her hair and its darkness cascaded over her shoulders. She leaned forward again, a hand on either thigh, elbows slightly akimbo. "Um, can I ask you something?"

"I guess."

"Well, listen. Answer carefully. A, B, or C. Doug, are you emotionally involved, as they say? In our relationship, I mean?"

He wanted to touch her face. Joni Mitchell was singing something about always being bound to someone.

She waited, fingers forming a steeple.

"So." He looked away. "I guess I *am* emotionally involved. Better yet, I'm not emotionally involved, but I love you. Does that make sense?"

"I guess." She moved to an armchair covered with a bedspread, lit a cone of incense and placed it in a miniature replica of an adobe house, her gestures delicate enough for a tea ceremony.

The music stopped.

"Okay," she said. "Here we go." She folded her hands. "This is how I feel, in a nutshell. You're my brother, Doug. I *like* to see it that way, it doesn't exclude anybody or anything." She took a deep breath. "Above all else, this is where I place my energy. It's open and it's high." She stopped. "What you think?"

He folded his own hands. "I think relationships, like writing, are transfers of energy."

She held up a finger. "Not so fast. One more thing, okay? I can't have a relationship, not the way people expect, and that doesn't only mean you, Doug. I have other work to do. Energy, as you know, is environmental, but force makes things happen." Smoke swirled from the tiny adobe chimney. She brought the tips of her fingers together. "Again. Putting aside wrong-thinking brought about by man's erroneous measure of time, I recognize we've vibrated in the presence of each other's energy over many lifetimes." She grinned. "Quite a mouthful, huh? But—to continue—I think we're both against imprisoning thoughts and possessive relationships."

"Of course," he said.

They brewed two cups of tea and sat in the darkness.

✻

Sometimes I bicycle along the Platte River. The water, icy but still flowing, raises my spirits. Sometimes, when the light's soft, in the late afternoons, I see her walking on the other side of the river, near Mile-High Stadium, a slender waif-like figure, and she waves, her hair taking dominion over the last light. That's why I sway on the red hooked rug in the center of my room, my head angling toward the hallway, waiting for a voice from the invisible world.

*

"What is it, Doug?"

"It's a toy from the factory where I work. It has pointed ears, and it holds its head high, and it does absolutely nothing at all."

"Is it Snoopy?"

He laughed. "If that's what you want it to be. It's yours. You can make it dance the Snoopy dance, if you wish, or sleep with it, or put it in a box."

"Whatever."

"Whatever."

The muddy bayou behind her cottage, where he stayed alone, made its sluggish way through the countryside, like a great lazy serpent sloughing its skin. He stalked lush Louisiana fields, smoked cigarettes, counted the mice in the cottage. He explored deserted houses and antiquated sugar-cane mills, cautiously skirting trailers where oil-field workers lived with their families. Everywhere he heard the recoils of rifles: roughnecks, teaching their wives to shoot. When they left for rigs in the Gulf, they loaded shotguns and their wives nodded.

Before he returned to Denver, Annie danced by the bayou. Randy sat near the water and stroked Odessa. "You'll be sorry when she's gone, won't you, girl?" he asked, scratching the dog behind the ears. All men are brothers, he knew, and he tried to live by that creed, despite his quick temper and practical nature. Annie, his spiritual sister, wanted wisdom, the things the Buddha taught, and that was fine with him, so long as he could be with her. He loved her. That day, she stretched and leaped in moist grass, turned twice before touching ground. The sun sparkled on floating branches in the bayou. Two moss-draped oaks framed her stage. The three of them could have been alive anywhere.

One late afternoon, when the huge Louisiana sun was sinking like a lost world into the trees, Annie and Doug found four owl feathers next to a shotgun shell in a clearing. "Just because the shotgun shell is next to the feathers," he said, "doesn't mean the bird is dead."

She put her fingers to her forehead, shielding her eyes, and dropped her arms. "Maybe not, but did you have to put it into words?" They walked around the clearing and found maybe two dozen more feathers. She arranged them on her bed by order of size. "Would you like one? I'll give you one now and send you one later. We can leave the others for the mice," she said. "You know, placate them so they don't bite you?"

"Sure," he said, sheepish about his mouse fear. "Who else would want such a gift?"

"I don't know, though maybe mice would prefer strawberry sundaes."

"You've got to be kidding."

She looked incredulous, opening her mouth wide and raising her carefully-trimmed eyebrows. "Would I kid about a strawberry sundae?"

✳

The news is on the radio—war overseas, a visit to China, the death of a celebrity. It's time to take a break. Afternoon recess is over and I haven't budged from the chair. At the toy factory, toys are products, children consumers: consistency satisfies expectations. We have a suggestion-box, though, and I tell the box, every day I work, that we should make wind-up ballerinas and provide them with all necessary accessories.

I'm taking everything too seriously.

Some nights, lights blazing, I lie awake. Is there a superior being? Is the Earth an organism, conscious of design, each of us a cell? Am I my sense of wonder, my sense of play?

I've dismantled myself, trying to become whatever my inner being dictates, trying to vibrate on the same wavelength as Annie, but I'm still waiting.

It's late afternoon. Snow flurries are falling to the street. The sidewalks will be white. Imprints of little feet will surround the school.

As the children leave the schoolyard, I know what I can do: I can walk home beside them and stop at the ice cream parlor. I can stand in line (if there's a line on a day like this) until the man with the paper hat calls my number. I can order a strawberry sundae.

※

Doug gathered his pack, changed the oil in his Valiant and left Louisiana. Annie stayed with Randy. She had not told Doug they were married until he had noticed Randy's ring. The idea that she could leave the marriage without exactly leaving it, that legalisms had nothing to do with the secret counterworld all of them *really* lived in, was a fiction Annie and Doug both held to be true. Randy wasn't so sure. Annie left him soon after she decided not to come to Denver, but he still wears the ring, a gold band. If she ever decides to join Doug, he'll follow. How can he know the invisible world really exists, unless he's with her?

As Doug drove through Texas, a sudden blast of air from the defroster sent the owl feather drifting to the seat. Could that have been symbolic? he wondered. Maybe only symbols exist in the world, parading before us, disguised as ordinary experience. If that's true, he thought, I can wait for years. I've waited this long. Why not a little longer?

There's a dream he remembers all too clearly. Widow Annie lived with him in a ramshackle hut, surrounded by hundreds of people in hovels. Beyond the huts, they could see sugar-cane, wood-slatted trucks. Widow Annie faded. A curtain replaced her at the window. "We'll be happy here," Doug told the girl who threw Annie's things into the street, but a hairy fist smashed the pane of glass and waved a lead pipe. He woke, sweating.

※

I'd like to buy a wind-up Jehovah's Witness and send it waddling down the street, saying its predictable things. Wouldn't that be nice, a toy everybody would know what to make of, that could tell us why the world is filled with trouble? In the meantime, I wait for the next dance, the next passionate longing to whirl me away from myself. I'm tired of playfulness, tired of trying to name things.

I guess I should've wanted something. Something specific, I mean. I guess I should've wanted something from the beginning. Something tangible, I mean. When I was with Annie, I pretended desire had nothing to do with the world, that love just happened. People got together according to cosmic intentions.

So. Perhaps it's not too late.

I want a strawberry sundae.

✳

Doug bundled up. "Good-bye, Tangle. See you."

The hallway smelled like food. The girl next door was cooking dinner and the aroma was lovely. The stairs creaked as he went down. The single bulb on the ceiling in the foyer was brightly burning. Across the street, janitors left the school—vague shadows in the dark snow.

How refreshing it was to walk alone on the streets! There were bare trees with limbs like spiderwebs, old houses two floors tall with gingerbread trim, toys on some of the porches. And footprints! They disappeared after a while in the falling snow, but he followed them as long as he could.

GOING WEST

In a science-fiction story I read last year when Audrey and I were separated, an Earthling and a Martian meet in a time warp. Each believes the other's civilization is in ruins, or never existed. They stand perplexed in the Martian desert, sand swirling around them, and try finally to clasp hands in a gesture of goodwill. But their fingers slide through each other like the blades of a skate through ice.

Recently, housebound with the two kids in the dead of a blizzard for three days, I had the television, the kids their Leggo blocks, Audrey her sewing. But how many reruns of "M*A*S*H" can you stomach, especially with the sound turned up to drown out Margaret's tantrums and Stevie's new obsession with percussion instruments? Leggos were scattered over five rooms and Audrey was reduced to thumbing through magazines.

I raised the white flag. "Let's go find the sun," I announced, clicking off "The Dukes of Hazzard" and dropping on all fours to reach under the couch for Stevie's long-lost farm implement hat. He wouldn't travel without it. Otherwise, the world might find out about his cowlick. "Licked by a cow, licked by a cow," he repeated, clamping the tiny hat on his head, as though capping a geyser.

"Is that what he gets at nursery school?" I asked Audrey.

"Beats me," she said, still in her magazine. "The sun?"

"I figure we head south," I said. "I'll check the weather channel first."

I pulled out the big suitcase.

"Hey," she said, Margaret half-stuffed into her snowsuit, "what's this? I thought we were going for a ride." The plastic on our picture window had bubbled. Only an occasional pickup or four-wheel drive ventured out. A single plow worked its way down our street, wind swirling snowdust around it. Its driver had on a moonsuit of metallic silver. Long tubes as thick as a forearm led from his glass compartment to the plow's hot engine.

"I'll warm up the car and shovel the drive," I said. "Why don't you gather up some cassettes, make a thermos of coffee?"

✳

On the road the kids fell asleep, Stevie cuddled against Margaret's carseat. Audrey loosened their seat belts and covered them with a plaid quilt. Every time I glanced in the rearview mirror I thought of Scotland. "We're not going to stop until we find it, you know."

"That so?" Audrey said. "That means we never go back." The interstate was dry and plowed, with great dirty drifts tilting toward us on either side, snow swirling across in fine sandy layers. Everything was white.

We went west. The weather channel had mentioned a warmer front in that direction. The temperature did rise a few degrees, but after three hours the sky was still slate-gray, the horizon still the color of dirty laundry.

At a gas station an attendant, stocky as a steer, grunted when I asked his advice. "Let me get this straight," he said, lips downturned, gruffness quick-frozen, shipped from the Scandinavian tundra. "You not going anywhere? You just looking for the sun?"

"You bet," I said, signing the credit slip. "Am I going to find it?"

He considered my question. "Not once it gets dark."

At the motel I pulled out the map and spread it on one of the two rumpled beds. For a few minutes I talked about routes, figuring mileage and driving time, leaning close to the unfolded, crinkled paper to make out place names: Medina, Williston, Miles City, towns of mud engineers, farm implement manufacturers, owners of greasy diners.

109

I folded the map and jammed it into the slip pocket of the nylon suitcase. Stevie, twice Margaret's age, was teaching her how to turn the second bed into a trampoline. Audrey had her hair down, one arm outstretched like a guard rail near Margaret, who landed on her back and squealed.

"Maybe we ought to forget about it," I said.

Neither of us fell in love with anyone else. "We don't have a marriage anymore," I remembered shouting. "We have a family." In some ways an affair would have made sense. But Audrey was busy with two kids and I was too tired to be interested. Instead, I rented an apartment near the plant where I worked.

"I have one baby crying for a bottle and another screaming for a bath," Audrey would say over the phone. "When the hell you coming home?" The line would go quiet. "You're deserting me, aren't you?"

"No," I would say, tapping the windowsill. "I've been working fourteen hours. Don't you appreciate that?"

I sat on the balcony, some nights, once it got warm, and drank, and watched the stars.

✳

"I'm sorry," she said. "Did I disappear in the middle of your plans?"

"No, it's not that." I shrugged, running my fingers over the pasteboard cover of a Gideon Bible. I opened it at random: "Will you judge them?" I read. "Will you judge them, son of man? Then confront them with the detestable practices of their father and say hem." Stevie took Margaret into one corner of the motel room. Beneath a picture of mountains, all rosy in the late afternoon, he tried to change her disposable diaper. She started crying when he snatched it and waved it like a flag. "Hey!" I shouted.

"Were you serious?" Audrey asked later, the kids asleep. She rested her chin on her knees, still steaming from the shower. "Because the trip is a good idea, Rod. The weather's okay now, not dangerous. What the hell."

The empty thermos floated in the basin. Water dripped from the faucet. "Thinking about it makes it weird," I said. "Going after the sun is something a kid might do."

She shifted on the bed. "So what? Weird is good. People up here, they're afraid to be weird. You start to think the Nazis won the war." She sipped the last of the day's hot coffee. "Let's move," she said. "Let's get back down South, maybe Louisiana, where people aren't so bored with their lives."

The next day we passed a couple of old missile silos, concrete slabs in the middle of nowhere surrounded by heavy-duty fences. We peered into the heavens now and then, beyond the snow and stubble, but the flat fields stretched for miles. We could hardly tell in the mist where ground stopped and sky began.

"Audrey?"

"Hmm?" A magazine jostled on her lap.

"What happened with us?"

"You want an answer?" she asked. Far ahead, on the road, someone flailed his arms, as though doing side-straddle hops. "What the heck is that?" Stevie wondered. "A midget?"

"He's just far away," I said, slowing down. A car had its hood up a half mile or so beyond the waving figure. And then I saw the hair falling from her knitted cap. "She's had a breakdown." On the upper plains, you feel you've fallen off the edge of the world. Houses, grain silos, even people take on a two-dimensional tiltiness. The sight of a polar bear lumbering across desolate fields would be disorienting but not entirely unexpected, while the woman, snowsuited, waving her arms, shocked me to attention.

She ran toward our car. I snapped on the emergency lights and inched to the roadside. Shoulders slumped, she stopped several feet from us. "Wait here," I said absurdly, zipping up my coat.

We talked on the edge of the flat snowy fields, and I knew from her tone of voice, even before I made out the words, that her companion had left the car. It's the one thing you never do in such weather, not ever. You pack slow-burning candles, sleeping bags, high-energy grub in case of breakdown. But leaving the car is taboo. The cold makes you tired, sluggish; not even an arctic expedition would have better than even odds if the wind started up again.

The skin on her cheekbones was purple and raw, tears of frustration frozen beneath her eyes. Her old car could have been propped up with a pair of two-by-fours.

"Have you seen him?" she shouted.

He was dead. I found out next day. The two of them had a fight. He decided to cool off, fast, in his windbreaker, and got frozen against a fencepost. He looked alive in the picture—jeans snagged on barbed wire, one hand scratching at his scalp.

Over her shoulder a squad car U-turned across a strip of neutral ground. Lights flashing, it pulled beside her disabled vehicle. My eyes stung in the wind as I pointed to the officer. She turned to see the hooded bear-like figure walk to her car, peer inside, then spot us.

She squeezed my arm. "Thanks." We stared at each other. She had pale determined features, lips indrawn, eyes hard-set. Under different circumstances, I might have found her quite lovely.

Before I could offer a lift, she was halfway to the squad car, running bow-legged for balance.

✳

"The police are out on a day like this," I said, with authority, but Audrey and I exchanged glances.

Later we stopped again. In the distance we saw a mountain range. "We've gone far enough, haven't we?" Stevie asked.

"Besides," added Audrey, "I think I see the sun."

Huddled around the car, we argued. In the far distance, through a geometry of high-powered telephone lines and scaffolding, there was something, though it provided little heat or light, just the barest trace of a disk, something noticeable only because it was different from what had been there before. It was like the way you can tell in a dark room, by heartbeat or breathing, whether you're with people you care for or not.

Alan Davis, a founding editor of *American Fiction*, grew up in Louisiana, where his parents and six brothers and sisters still reside. He now lives in Minnesota, where he chairs the English Department and directs creative writing at Moorhead State University. His fiction and nonfiction appear in such newspapers as the *Cleveland Plain-Dealer*, the *New York Times*, and the *San Francisco Chronicle*, and in such journals as *The Hudson Review*, *Kansas Quarterly*, and *The Quarterly*. "Match-Book," his weekly program of commentary on literature and the arts, can be heard on National Public Radio affiliates. He's received a scholarship from Breadloaf and a fellowship from the Minnesota State Arts Board. Currently, he is working on a second collection of stories and on two novels set in Louisiana.